Balthazar, the Black and Shining Prince

A Christmas Legend /

By Alvin Lester ben-Moring

Illustrated by John Gretzer

Balthazar,
the Black and Shining Prince

The Westminster Press

Philadelphia

Book Design by Dorothy Alden Smith

Published by The Westminster Press ®
Philadelphia, Pennsylvania

PRINTED IN THE UNITED STATES OF AMERICA

Library of Congress Cataloging in Publication Data

Ben-Moring, Alvin Lester, 1931–
    Balthazar, the black and shining prince.

    SUMMARY: An imaginary biography of Balthazar, the
black prince and the third of the Magi.
    1. Magi—Juvenile fiction. [1. Magi—Fiction]
I. Gretzer, John, illus. II. Title.
PZ7.B425Bal   [Fic]   74-8177
ISBN 0-664-32554-8

To the Memory of Miss Carrie Pringle

i

In the year that Caesar Augustus became "divine emperor" of the Roman Empire, Balthazar, the black and shining prince, finder and proclaimer of the Christ-child, was born. Ancient and noble Har'lem, the place of his birth, was a miraculously created city that lay almost due south of the ruins of Carthage in North Africa. Har'lem had been planned and laid out by flaming messengers of the one true God more than a century before.

At this early time, long before Balthazar's birth, the mighty Roman legions had already burst the boundaries of their empire. In the name of conquest, they had crossed the sea from Rome and the European continent. Great Carthage lay under their heavy attack and soon would be leveled to the ground. Salt would be plowed into her fields and vineyards so that for centuries to come nothing would grow, flower, or bear fruit in her soil. It would be known as the darkest hour in the history of that once-strong city. Yet out of that darkness a glimmer of light was beheld from the eternal beacon of hope. When that dreadful day of destruction came, a marvelous legend began to unfold. It was the legend of Har'lem—its first beginning and, at length, the heroic story of its black and shining prince.

The wondrous legend began as the Roman legions were preparing to destroy without mercy whatever was left of the already-dying city of Carthage. Each soldier had been issued five oil-soaked torches and a flint. Their commanders had given orders that the soldiers were to form themselves into units, march into the city, light the torches and burn everything still standing that could be burned. Six hours before the appointed time, the Angel of the Lord was sent by the Almighty himself to save the members of the royal house, their trusted servants, and a few chosen close friends. The Angel called together the four winds and gave them instructions.

The North Wind was ordered to blow upon the soldiers with bone-chilling blasts. This made the already cold air of the desert night even colder. The sudden drop in temperature slowed the bodily movements of the soldiers, making them uncomfortable and angry with their officers for having brought them to that place. As friend of the North Wind, the East Wind was instructed to catch the shouted words and orders coming from the mouths of the officers and captains and throw them away. This caused confusion and panic in the camps, for the troops were unable to hear or understand the commands given to them. Therefore the orders were impossible to carry out.

The West Wind was told to grant warm, tranquil protection for the royal refugees and their company. It was further to shield them from the combined scourge of the North and East winds. Finally, the South Wind was to provide passage for the rescued company. It was to lift them above the doomed city and move them swiftly, safely, and gently to a spot that the Angel of the Lord had already prepared. They were to ride comfortably upon the skirts of the South Wind and thus escape certain death.

All night they rode the swirling wind. At last the sense of motion calmed, and the sky travelers were gently lowered to the earth as dawn began to break on the horizon. The sky was misty, yet it shone like a rainbow with faint patches of green, gold, white, blue, red, and purest black. The shining warmth eased the fears of the refugees and soon sleep crept over them. When the four winds came to wake them, they stared in awe at the great miracle that surrounded them. A clearing had been cut in the dense jungle, and the nearby rivers had been brought together to form a shim-

8

mering lake. All of this beauty and wonder had been created by the very breath of the Angel of the Lord. As the refugees knelt in thankful prayer, a voice came to them, echoing from across the lake.

"You are among the chosen men of the earth. The day shall come when a prince of this city shall walk the earth in search of the Glory of the Lord. He shall find it and proclaim it to all the world. Let this city evermore be known as Har'lem. Let this your city of Har'lem be a kingdom of peace and justice. Forget not the one true God, who saved you from the Romans. Remember to give him continual praise."

The voice was gone as suddenly as it had come, but the words of the Angel of the Lord had taken root in their hearts.

In the years that followed, the city of Har'lem grew in size and wealth, and its people maintained their faithfulness to the one true God. The Angel's promise of a holy prince was never forgotten, but generation after generation of royal sons were born, and none grew up to fulfill the prophecy. It was not until the fifth generation that this hope was revived. An unusual prince was born into the royal home. He was given the name Balthazar, which even as a child he bore with great pride. He seemed to grow with unusual intensity in boyish grace, and he asked endless questions that startled his elders. His mother the queen secretly hoped in her heart that he would indeed be the prophesied prince from whom mankind could benefit. The teachers of the royal children and those of the noble families were attracted by his strength, obedience, and courage. Most of the people of Har'lem felt that his behavior was praiseworthy and unrivaled by any other sons of the kingdom.

There were yet other actions of young Prince Balthazar that set him apart from his companions. At times when boys of the realm would gather for sport, he would slip away to the lake's edge and dream of the secrets that he thought were being whispered by the winds. Soon the dreams became prayers. As his faith grew stronger the prayers became meditations. Also there was the secret cave high up on the treacherous mountain path, where he and his servant-friend Clitus would steal away whenever time would permit. Clitus had taken a blood oath never to tell Balthazar's secret and never to show anyone the cave. In that cave Balthazar slowly began to understand the meaning of the whispering winds of which he had dreamed. Though only a boy, he was the most religious of all who lived in Har'lem.

Balthazar's father, the king, was wise, rich, and good. He believed in justice and honesty. During his reign he was blessed with the privilege of building a shrine for the worship of the one true God. No one in Har'lem was sure what the one true God was like, for there were no images or pictures of him.

The king wanted to be sure that his warmhearted son would even be a better king than he had been. With satisfaction he watched Balthazar learn to ride and jump a horse. He watched him learn how to play kickball and how to throw the javelin. Balthazar was already the fastest runner for his age and excelled in elementary wrestling. When riding with his father to and from state functions he always sat tall and regally in the saddle, although his feet barely touched the stirrups. So, before Balthazar was twelve years old, his father the king decided that he would be sent to Spain for a more formal education and training. For Balthazar the choice was perfect, for at the University of Cádiz he was destined to meet two other youths who would become his friends and companions for life.

The formal school proved to be more difficult and challenging than the court school had been. The discipline of organized classes and small discussion groups with long hours of private study and research proved to be tedious. At times it was unbearable and even boring. The regimen was nonetheless necessary, since some of the young princes and nobles would be kings at ages seventeen, eighteen, or twenty. Wanting to please his parents, Balthazar studied almost everything. He studied the Greek and Latin languages. He studied arithmetic and higher mathematics. He read great philosophers while studying history and law. His favorite study was religion, because he wanted to know more about the one true God of his father, whom very few people seemed to know anything about at all.

Balthazar also studied the stars. He wondered about their being so high up and so very far away from the earth. Yet these "fiery holes in the blackened heavens," as he called them, seemed to have importance in the lives and affairs of men. Great ships ran their courses according to the stars. Farmers knew when to plant their seeds and harvest their crops according to the stars. Sorcerers and astrologers used the stars as omens whenever any strange event happened that could not be otherwise explained. For it was not the earth that moved; it was rather the stars, the moon, and the sun that moved. Therefore as points of reference, the stars were very important.

In addition to following all the disciplines of the mind, Balthazar was growing as an athlete. He had become the best horseman who had ever attended the school. He was good at gymnastics and excelled in the use of the sword as well as the small knife. He could run, jump, leap, climb, and do all kinds of tricks. He was admired everywhere he went and men looked up to him. He stood six feet tall; his skin was smooth, dark brown, almost black. His hair was thick and coarse, and it added to his appearance as a man who had to be taken seriously. The smile he bore automatically put everyone at ease; it would even make sad people happy. His manner of speech was sonorous and a little slow, but when he spoke, everyone listened, for he usually had something worthwhile to say. His teeth were white, like gleaming pearls, and when he smiled, all the women of the realm fell in love with him. Each of them wanted to marry him and bear his children, yet he had little time for them.

As he had done when he was a small boy, Balthazar spent much of his time alone. In those moments of quiet and peace when he deliberately went off by himself, he would say that he was looking for God. He would say that he was listening for God. He felt that if he could not hear God speak to him from the outside, with his ears, then perhaps he could hear God speaking within. Although he seemed to be at peace with himself, and many times proved to be good company in the presence of others, he had not found the absolute peace he was searching for.

"How does God speak to us?" he asked his teacher, Philo, the renowned Greek, one day.

"The Hebrew scriptures say that God is unapproachable," the teacher answered.

"Then how can we know when he speaks to us?" black Balthazar repeated.

"He speaks through various signs and wonders. It is he who usually approaches us, and not we him."

"Does God have a shape or a form?" the prince asked.

"Not as we know shape and form."

"How then do we know that he is not simply an invention of our minds?"

"Do you feel the wind blowing, Balthazar?" the teacher asked.

"Yes," the student answered. "I feel the wind."

"Where is it blowing?"

"It is blowing upon my face. See, it even moves my tunic as it blows."

"Can you see the wind, Balthazar?" the teacher asked once again.

"No," answered the prince, "I cannot see it."

"Yet you know it is blowing."

"I know because I feel it."

"That is the way the knowledge of God comes. One does not see it. One feels it, and in the feeling of it, one knows."

For a long time after the parting, Balthazar thought about what Philo had told him. Slowly but surely it began to make some sense to him. Leaving the courtyard where he and Philo had been talking, Balthazar went off to seek his two closest friends. They were princes like himself. One was handsome Prince Caspar, from Spain. He was olive-complexioned and only a hair's breadth shorter than Balthazar. His long, curly black hair hung down to his broad shoulders. Caspar's eyes were as black and bright as two marbles. He seemed actually to be able to look through people. The first time he saw Balthazar he said, "There goes a man and a prince whom I shall surely come to know and love." Caspar's father was king of Las Luces. As a powerful king, he was also a friend of Balthazar's father. His kingdom was under the loose control of an aging Roman governor who feared the prowess of the

Spaniards. Thus the kingdom was left to govern itself so long as taxes were paid to the Romans.

Balthazar's other friend was also a prince, and he came from a place called Britain. Melchior was his name. He had long light hair, beautiful steel-blue eyes, and a fair, pinkish complexion. He was always complaining about the heat. It was never quite cold enough for him. Even on days that made Balthazar and Caspar uncomfortably cool, he was still too warm. Balthazar and Caspar found him strange and wondered if there were other white people in the world like Melchior. The British prince spoke of the way many of his people yet lived in huts, in woods and marshes. They fought tribal wars, and carried off their enemies if they wanted to. Sometimes they ate the children of the defeated ones. Balthazar and Caspar laughed at this.

The three princes were almost inseparable. During those days at the university they were seen together most of the time. They laughed, played, sang, studied, and even drank wine together. Life for them was to be lived to its fullest, and not simply to be talked about like an arithmetic problem to be solved. They used to take long walks and rides through the Spanish countryside. Where they found people in need or having problems, the three friends would do their best to be of help. There was no need to tell others that they were future kings—people seemed to sense this. Very soon their comrades at school were calling them the three kings.

Later that evening, the three comrades were in their large living quarters with their tutor, Philo. They were following up the question Balthazar had asked that afternoon. None of them realized that the questions they raised and the answers they sought would have far-reaching consequences.

"I remember reading about God becoming man," Caspar said.

"Whom did you read?" Melchior asked.

"One of the great Greek teachers. Plato, I think."

"And what exactly did he say?"

"He said that if God wanted to make himself known, the only way he could do so was to become a man."

"I read that too," Balthazar told them.

"Do you believe it?" Melchior asked again.

"I think I do. It seems believable."

13

"In what way?" the British prince questioned. "Not that I don't believe it."

"Look, suppose as a man you wanted to communicate with a colony of ants," Caspar said.

"Might be a good idea," Melchior replied. "They are good to eat, you know."

"Be serious." Caspar smiled. "Suppose you wanted to communicate with them, not eat them. How would you do it?"

"Certainly I would have to find a way."

"But what way? Stop fooling and answer Caspar's question," said Balthazar, who himself was smiling.

"I don't know. I guess I would have to learn their language—that is, if they have one," Melchior replied.

"All right, then what?" Caspar was persistent.

"Then I would bend down and talk with them, telling them who I was and what I wanted."

"But would that be enough?" Philo questioned the Briton. The three students knew now that Caspar's original question was very important.

"They might be frightened by the immense difference in your sizes," Balthazar suggested.

"Then I would have to make an adaptation." Melchior wanted to demonstrate that he too could be serious.

"And what would be the best way to do that?"

Melchior cupped his large chin in his stout fist, resting his elbow on the rough table. He was silently considering his teacher's last question. There was quiet in the room. Only the sputtering wick of the oil lamp could be heard. Melchior raised his golden head, looked at his comrades and his teacher, and said with authority, "I guess I would have to become an ant."

"I agree, for I too read what Caspar read." Balthazar came to his feet. "And, at the time I read it I remembered what one of the Hebrew prophets wrote."

"Which one?" asked Philo, who was proud of his students.

Balthazar looked at his notes. "The prophet Isaiah. He said, 'Unto us a child is born, unto us a son is given.' "

"Who is the child, and whose son is he?" Melchior asked.

"I think the prophet answers that in an indirect way," Balthazar continued. "He says, 'and the government shall be upon his shoulder.' "

"That doesn't say too much," Caspar replied. "Why, we don't even know what is meant by 'government.' "

"But we are given clues," Balthazar maintained. Reaching for a scroll, and spreading it out before him, he continued excitedly, "Listen to this: 'And his name shall be called Wonderful, Counselor, The mighty God, The everlasting Father, The Prince of Peace.' Now tell me, my brothers, do we know of any kingdom anywhere in the world where the princes and kings claim titles such as these? Well, do we?"

The room became hushed. Caspar and Melchior looked at each other. Philo scratched his half-gray, half-bald head. He knew most of the kingdoms of the world, but he did not know of any that had rulers or princes who claimed titles such as the ones Balthazar had read from the scroll.

" 'The mighty God, The everlasting Father, The Prince of Peace,' " Caspar repeated. "If these words were spoken by a prophet, then they are prophecy. And if they are prophecy, then either they have come to pass—"

"Or the time is yet to come. They are yet to happen," Melchior interrupted.

"But how, or when?" old Philo asked.

"Soon," answered Balthazar, who felt a stirring in his bones.

"How do you know?" Caspar asked seriously.

Melchior and Philo looked at Balthazar curiously.

Balthazar smiled. "Like the blowing of the wind, I simply feel it." Outside their windows the wind blew fiercely, lightning flashed, and thunder rolled through the heavens.

ii

THE NEXT FEW DAYS AFTER THE NIGHT OF THE DISCUSSION AND THE very big storm were strange ones. There seemed to be a general unrest almost everywhere. It seemed as if the devil had taken over nature. The wind was blowing harder than usual. Trees were knocked down; streams and brooks overflowed. The sky was dark, and when the sun shone it looked burnished and gloomy. Thick, smoky clouds shaped like bulls moved angrily across the heavens. They butted into other clouds with fury. Lightning flashed, striking frequently. Thunder rolled, and buckets of water came pouring from the skies. It was almost impossible to get anywhere. Roads were washed away, and paths were choked with brush, brambles, and briers. This made things difficult for both man and beast.

The three comrades stayed close to their university home and continued to consider the coming of the promised child with their teacher. The wise old Philo did not always answer their questions directly. He would sometimes ask them questions in return. This would make them think for themselves. It also made their answers more meaningful.

"Don't the Hebrew prophets say other things about this coming God-child?" Melchior asked.

"One of them said that he would be born in Judah," Caspar

17

told them. "It is said that even though Bethlehem is the least of all the cities of Judah, from there would come an everlasting king."

"There is that word again—everlasting," Balthazar said, beating his own fist with an open hand.

"But is a small town the proper place for a king to be born?" Philo asked. "Is not the great city of Jerusalem a far more suitable place? Jerusalem is the traditional place of kings in that land."

"Then why does the prophet refer to Bethlehem?" Balthazar asked.

"Philo is right," Caspar said. "Jerusalem would be more logical. Maybe he will be born in Jerusalem and for some untold reason will have to go to Bethlehem."

"Once in Bethlehem, he could 'come forth' again," Melchior said, for he agreed with Caspar.

"Even if you are correct, that doesn't solve the heart of this riddle," Balthazar maintained.

"And what is that?" asked Melchior.

"He is proclaimed to be an everlasting king," said Balthazar. "That would mean that he cannot and will not be an ordinary person like ourselves."

"What do you mean?" Philo asked.

"Melchior, Caspar, and I are princes," said Balthazar. "When our fathers die, we shall be kings. We cannot make the claim of being everlasting. We are human and we shall die, all of us. But this king will be everlasting; therefore, he must be different."

"Balthazar has to be correct," Melchior agreed. "I never would have thought about it that way."

"Nor I," Caspar said.

"Now we must see if we can discover the exact time and place," Melchior declared.

"If indeed it is in our lifetime," said Philo, who was feeling his old age.

"It has to be in our lifetime!" Caspar's fist struck the table.

"We must separate," Balthazar said. "We must each go to our home and there work at the thing we each do best. Melchior, you must consult the stars. You must discover what they have foretold in the past and what they appear to foretell of the future. There

18

are famed astrologers in your father's court. You must employ their help. Perhaps even the heavens will give a sign."

"That sounds like a good idea," Melchior said. "If the person coming is to be an everlasting king, then the heavens would surely say something about it. At least they should."

"What shall I do?" Caspar asked.

"The thing you do best," said Balthazar. "Your father's court is known for its sages and magicians. Question them, find out what they know about anything similar to what we have discovered. Don't leave out anything, no matter how small it seems. When you have finished, rejoin Philo here. And you, Philo, dear Philo, continue to search the holy writings, and compare your findings with what the seers and Caspar will tell you."

"What if I discover something very important?" Melchior asked.

"We'll use the message-carrying homing pigeons."

"Again, an excellent idea." Caspar grinned broadly. "Why didn't I think of that?"

"We can also use the homing pigeons to send word to each other," Melchior added.

"And what will you do?" Philo asked Balthazar.

"I am going back home to the mountains of Har'lem. There I shall meditate, pray, and ask the one true God for a sign. I will hope for some sense of direction, or some definite clue. When I am ready, all of you must be ready to come to me at once. We shall share our gathered information. There is no doubt in my mind that we shall then know what to do."

That same day, each of the princes sent a message to his father by homing pigeon, asking that things be readied for him when he arrived. Two days later the three companions embraced each other and separated. Each traveled his own route for home.

It took Caspar only twelve days to reach his home in Las Luces. He then was able to get to work first. He followed Balthazar's suggestions to the letter. Working together with Balthazar and Melchior made him happy. There was joy and excitement in all the things he did. Caspar spent days and nights with the many magicians of the Spanish court. He spoke with the seers and the astrologers who were there. Everything that seemed important to the quest he wrote down. At times he would secretly leave the palace in order to talk with the magicians and the seers who were not approved by his father's court. From them he learned of an interesting Egyptian myth that had to do with an everlasting king. This king's name was Osiris. Men had adored and worshiped Osiris, who promised them everlasting life. But his followers and his religion had disappeared in the course of time. Caspar was amused by that last fact. The one thing he did not forget was to spend at least an hour a day attending to his own prayers and meditation. Balthazar had shown him how to do even that.

Melchior had to go farther in order to get home to Britain. The messenger he had sent had arrived a whole week before he did. What he saw when he got there pleased him. His father had exceeded the written requests by going to the trouble of borrowing famed astrologers from across the great northern waters that froze during the wintertime. Using all their knowledge, they set about studying the stars. Every well-known historical event was related to the stars and their positions in the heavens. The studies showed that two highly significant events had occurred in the course of history. To Melchior's amazement one of these happened on a day when the sun shone for almost twenty-four hours straight.

"My goodness!" Melchior bolted upright. "You mean without there being any night?"

"That's right," one seer told him. "There had been no night at all for almost twenty-four hours. What night there was lasted less than one full hour."

"That surely was an omen," Melchior said, as though lost in thought. "But you said there were two things. What was the other?"

"Well, my prince, they also found that some eight hundred years later, for some unexplained reason, the sun had actually moved backward for a little while, about ten degrees on the sun dial."

"Impossible!" shouted the British prince.

"No, my lord, the sun usually rises in the east and travels to the west, where it sinks under the earth. On the special day of which I speak the sun reversed its course. For some unexplained reason it moved backward over the way it had come."

"In other words," said a second seer, "that event too had added to the length of the day, though not so much as in the first case."

"Did the sun behave differently in each case?" Melchior asked.

"Yes, my lord. In the first case it seemed not to move at all. In the second case it did move, but the movement was in reverse."

A smile crept across Melchior's face. He thought to himself, I wonder if Balthazar and Caspar know about this.

Meanwhile, black Prince Balthazar had reached his home in Africa. His parents, the King and Queen of Har'lem, were happy to see him. He told his father what had happened at the university and why he had returned home.

"Perhaps I can put the pieces of this puzzle together," he told his father.

"You must do as you see fit, my son. Someday you will be king. There won't be much time for personal things then. A good king must be responsible for his subjects and the kingdom. Your mother and I support you in this quest."

"Thank you, my father," said the prince.

That first night home Balthazar had a very strange dream. In the dream he saw himself standing outside what appeared to be a temple, a palace, or both. Its walls were so high they seemed to disappear up into the clouds. The gates of the temple-palace walls were shining and seemed to be covered with transparent gold overlaid with the purest mother-of-pearl you would ever see. He wanted to get into the temple-palace but there seemed to be no way. Being outside gave him a feeling of loneliness. It was almost as if he was the only man in the world. His heart was heavy, not with sadness, but with a longing. He was hungering and thirsting for something he needed deep down within.

How can I find meaning for my life? he said to himself. The thought that he would one day be a king did not occur to him. The question came at him again. This time there was more to it. How can I find meaning for my life—in service to the one true God? He smiled when he realized that the second part of the question had in it the seed of the answer. Frustratedly he looked up at the doors, which still seemed to offer no way of entering.

Suddenly a voice from nowhere and everywhere spoke to him. "Look behind you," it said. Balthazar turned quickly and there he saw a well. The twelve stones that surrounded the opening of the well also seemed to be made of pearl. He made his way slowly over to the well. At the top there was a bucket made of gold. Around its handle was tied a silver rope. "Lower the bucket, draw up some water and drink," the voice told him. He did so and found that it was the sweetest, coolest, purest water he had ever seen or tasted. The more he drank, the more he wanted. When at last he had drunk his fill, he put the bucket back where he had found it. As the bucket touched the top of the well he realized the answer to his question. At the moment he thought to speak it, he heard the voice again confirming what he already knew. "Your way shall be to discover where He is to be born and to point that way to the world."

Balthazar awoke with a start. His dark brown body was covered with sweat. Joy so filled his heart that he thought it would burst wide open. Hurriedly he went off to the king's council chamber, where he wrote brief messages reporting his dream to Melchior and to Caspar. These were tied to the legs of two of the fast-flying homing pigeons that Melchior and Caspar had exchanged with him just for this purpose. He set the birds free to return to their royal homes in Britain and Spain. Then, pleased with himself, he set out for a ride on his famous horse, Black Spirit.

This horse had been a gift to Balthazar from the people of Har'lem to mark his tenth birthday. Black Spirit had a coat as black as coal and as shiny as silk. He was the fastest, smartest, and strongest horse in the kingdom. In many ways the horse was as close a companion to Balthazar as any human being. They had been together for a long time and had learned to trust each other. In almost every way they understood one another.

The day that Balthazar had chosen to go riding, the sky was a deep blue with only wisps of white, fleecy clouds. The sun was shining bright and strong. Yet there was a wind blowing. This wind seemed to come out of nowhere and seemed to be going nowhere. It reminded him of the three days he and his companions

22

had experienced at the university during the great storm. Stretching in the saddle, he scanned the heavens for signs of coming rain. There were none. An uneasiness settled over him. Even Black Spirit appeared troubled as he struggled to stay on the mountain path. Balthazar was headed for a favorite spot of his high up on the mountain. It was the spot that only he and his faithful servant Clitus knew about—the cave they had secretly shared since childhood. From the cave's entrance one could look out across the plains and see the whole of the kingdom.

The higher up they went, the stronger the wind became. Balthazar thought he heard a voice in the wind say to him, "You shall not go; you shall not go." Without warning, the air grew cold and the wind blew harder, picking up bits of sand and gravel and stinging Balthazar's skin. Even Black Spirit neighed and whinnied in protest. Coming to a very sharp turn in the path, the great horse stumbled and fell. An evil gust of wind tumbled both horse and rider. Balthazar went sprawling head over heels in front of the horse. There was nothing before him to break his fall, so he was thrown off the sheer hillside. He landed in a tree, but with force so great that he continued to fall. Rocks rushed up to meet him; sand blinded his eyes, and his head was gashed by a jutting rock. Bouncing off more jagged rocks, he landed on a small ledge as if he were only a bag of sand. Everything was hushed except the wind, which seemed to laugh a devilish laugh.

Black Spirit secured his own footing. He frantically looked for a way to get down to his injured master, who was not moving. The horse tried this way and that; but no way was possible. There was only one thing he could do. Pulling all his strength and courage together, he started for home.

The evil wind blew against the great horse, throwing sand into his eyes, biting into his skin. Several times, Black Spirit fell, but love for his master made him determined that nothing would keep him from doing what he had to do. When the horse finally arrived at the palace, he was covered with dirt and blotches of blood. Balthazar's personal servant, Clitus, saw the animal come in riderless. When he approached the black stallion he saw that it had been spooked and was trembling. Clitus ran for the king and the other servants.

23

"Balthazar must be hurt," the king cried in dismay.

The horse continued to rear and paw at the ground.

"He probably wants to show us where the prince is, your highness," the young servant said.

The king turned to his other servants and shouted a command. "Quick! Make ready my chariot and fetch the royal doctor. We must go and search for my son."

As soon as the king had spoken, the servants moved quickly to obey. In a short time they were all ready and set out to find Balthazar. They galloped across the plains and into the foothills, stirring up dust as they went. The wind tried to hold them back, but could not. The king and Black Spirit were determined to get to Balthazar. When they arrived at the place where he had fallen, they could see Balthazar still lying on that small ledge below. Since he was not moving, they could not tell whether the prince was dead or alive.

"We must use a rope. Clitus, you will go down, secure him, and bring him up."

"As you command, my king," the strong Clitus answered.

The other servants readied the ropes. Clitus tied one rope around himself, and the other servants helped ease him over the side and down the steep, ragged face of the mountain. Several times he bumped and scraped himself, but he was determined to get to his master. When he got to the ledge, he saw that Balthazar was alive, but barely. He could see that several of the prince's bones were broken, but could not tell how bad the internal injuries might be. Another servant was lowered over the side to help Clitus. Working together, they prepared a body brace and a pulley so that Balthazar could be drawn up to the top of the ledge. Those at the top did the pulling. It was slow, hard work to rescue the prince, but with the help of Black Spirit they were able to do it. At the top, the royal doctor examined the broken and bleeding prince. He shook his black woolly head from side to side.

"I'm afraid to move him, your Majesty," the doctor told the king. "I'm afraid it is grave—the wounds are terribly serious."

"But what can we do?" asked the king.

"We'll have to find a place of shelter nearby."

"There's nothing closer than the palace. We'll have to move

him there." There seemed to be no choice.

"If it is your command, sire, then I shall have to obey," the doctor told him. "But if we move him that far, I cannot make any prediction except that probably, by morning, he will die."

The doctor's voice was sad and grave. The king looked at the stilled body of his favorite son, not knowing what to do. The wind could be heard again still blowing and sounding like evil laughter.

"Your Majesty, if it pleases the king, I will speak." Clitus had been brushing dirt from himself and licking some of the dirt from his little cuts and scrapes. Now he paused.

"What is it, Clitus?"

"I know of a cave not far from here. The prince and I have come here often. It has been his place of meditation and prayer. We discovered it when we were boys. I have been sworn to secrecy and took a blood oath never to reveal its location, but I know the prince will forgive me. There are torches there, a table, a few changes of clothing, sometimes food, and a bed."

"You must lead us to this place, Clitus, for my son must not die."

Clitus mounted his horse and led the company slowly toward the cave that he and Balthazar had known about and secretly used over the years. It proved to be only a short distance away. The king and the physician felt it to be most suitable. It was a rather large cave. The entrance was nearly hidden by the growth of brush and shrubs. It had a very high ceiling that made it look almost like the inside of a great temple. As Clitus had told them, there were torches, hanging along the wall. There was a large table upon which Balthazar was laid, and there was a bed. The doctor had brought a large supply of oils, wine, and dressings, which he needed to tend wounds. While the king himself held the torch for light, the doctor worked. First he cleaned the wounds with wine. Then he applied oil to those that he could. Those that were deeper he cleaned out and sewed up.

Although Balthazar moaned and groaned through all of this, he did not wake up. Several of his ribs were broken, and there was a very deep and long wound in his side. The doctor had to push the flesh back into the gash so that the healing could be complete.

He bound up the body with cloths where he could. Then he set the bones, using assorted pieces of wood for splints as they were needed. When he had finished at last, the doctor once again shook his head and asked the king to stand off to the side. In the presence of Clitus he spoke. "Your Majesty, I think we have taken care of the worst of it. There is one thing, however, that you ought to know."

"And what is that?" the king asked.

"The wound in his side. I don't know how it will heal. It could be already infected and poisonous. If that is so, then he will certainly die."

"Is there nothing more you can do?" the king demanded.

"Not for the present. I shall stay here with him until we know more. He must be moved to that bed and no further."

"So be it," the king said with finality. "Clitus, you shall stay here as my son's guardian. You shall bring me word of any and every change. If there is anything you and the doctor need from the palace, send me word. I will leave a man here to act as messenger. You shall remain at my son's side until he is well, or until he dies."

"Do not think of him dying, my lord," Clitus said, kneeling before his king.

"You shall have everything you need here. There shall be food, wine, fruit, and all the herbs and medicines the doctor shall prescribe. I shall also send clean cloths to bind his wounds. He is my son and must be given every chance to live."

The king left and sent back everything he had promised. Through the late afternoon and evening, Balthazar never moved nor stirred. It hardly appeared that he was breathing. If the alert and skillful doctor had not placed his ear to the black prince's chest from time to time, he would not have known that there was yet a flicker of life in the badly injured body.

Clitus built a small fire at one end of the cave in order to prepare a meal for the doctor, the messenger, and himself. Balthazar had not awakened. The doctor thought it best to let him sleep and gain whatever strength he could.

Evening wore on into night. While the doctor and the messenger were asleep on pallets, Clitus thought he had been awakened by a noise coming from Balthazar. Quickly jumping up from his sleeping place on the floor, he approached the bed of his young master and saw that the prince was covered with sweat. He was moving his head from side to side as though in a fever. Deep within the fever there was a vision. Something was happening, for Balthazar began to speak without waking up. The frightened Clitus listened, trying to hear every word. "How can I find meaning for my life in service to you, O one true God?" Balthazar was saying. "How can I find meaning for my life in service to you?"

Silence answered the feverish prince. Then, ever so slowly, the cave itself began to glow. The light, though imperceptible at first, soon changed from a glow to a kind of clouded mist. That clouded mist took on the shape of a chariot wheel and the wheel began to turn around and around. As it turned, it also became bigger and bigger. Gradually it seemed to fill the whole cave, covering the places where Balthazar lay, where Clitus stood, frightened out of his mind, and where the doctor and the messenger yet lay sleeping. Balthazar repeated the questions from out of his fever for the third time. "How can I find meaning for my life in service to you, O one true God?" Still he did not wake up. Suddenly within the big wheel as it turned there appeared another, smaller chariot wheel, which was blue in color. The smaller wheel began to turn—in the opposite direction. From out of that wheel there came a voice that Clitus himself heard. It had a deep, musical sound, pleasant to the ear, and it made his heart beat strongly. "You must discover where my Son is to be born," said the voice. "You must discover where my Son is to be born. You must discover that place and point the way for the entire world." As soon as the voice stopped speaking, the cave was flooded with a light that was brighter than the day, yet so soft that it did not hurt Clitus' eyes. The very cave itself seemed to open up and become larger. The roof raised itself up higher, and the walls became wider. In the place of the one big whirling, misty chariot wheel with the smaller blue wheel turning inside, there were now six large whirling wheels and six smaller blue wheels turning in the opposite direction within them. Clitus' throat became choked. He could not speak. There was nothing he could do or say. Words would not form in his mouth.

The wheels rose higher and higher in the cave and presently two things happened almost at once. Balthazar appeared to have been immediately healed, and he sat up in his bed looking around the cave, which had now seemingly become a huge throne room. Secondly, the cave had indeed become a throne room, but the top of the throne could not be seen. Only the base of the throne was visible, and that was of solid gold and covered with pearls, diamonds, and other precious jewels. The wheels continued to whirl and arranged themselves in the form of a circle, which moved around the throne. Now Balthazar stood, wrapped only in the cloths that bound his wounds. He held a jeweled sword in his hand. As he faced the great golden throne with its jeweled designs, he realized that he had never seen anything on earth like it. The ground began to shake, and the walls of the cave-temple began to quake, but neither Balthazar nor Clitus felt any danger of the earth splitting or opening. Then, at the base of the throne, they saw what seemed to be the lower folds of a royal robe. The strange cloth was richer, fuller, freer flowing, yet unlike any fabric either of the young black men had ever seen. A sweet-smelling fragrance, like the mixture of incense and perfume, filled the whole cave and stuffed their nostrils. The scent made them both feel vibrantly alive. It smelled like the very first day of all the seasons poured into one. With that smell came a feeling of weightlessness and a sense of timelessness.

The crash of thunder that followed nearly split their eardrums. In a moving, blinding flash of lightning, the six wheels turned into six angels—the most beautiful, yet the strangest creatures either Balthazar or Clitus had ever seen. These creatures, messengers of the One who sat upon the throne, were magnificent to behold. The first angel was red, the second green, the third blue, the fourth gold, the fifth black, and the last angel was white. Not only was each of them different in color, but each had six wings, and each wing was also different in color. One wing was red, another green, a third blue, the fourth gold, the fifth black, and the sixth white. With two wings they covered their beautiful faces; with two wings they covered their beautiful feet; and with two wings they flew. They moved back and forth, up and down, around and around the great gold and jeweled throne. They chanted a most glorious song. Its melody was so sweet that Balthazar and Clitus thought their hearts would break.

The angels sang:

> "Holy, Holy, Holy,
> Lord God of hosts,
> Heaven and earth are full of thy glory:
> Glory be to thee, O Lord Most High."

They sang this song three times. Then, quietly and slowly, the room seemed to spin and turn. Clitus looked at Balthazar, whose face seemed transformed already into that of the king he would one day become. The doctor and the messenger were still asleep, but Clitus longed for morning.

WHILE BALTHAZAR WAS LYING INJURED, CASPAR IN SPAIN AND
Melchior in far Britain received his message about the vision that
had appeared to the black prince on his first night at home. He
had told them of the voice directing him to go forth in order to
discover where "He" was to be born. Balthazar had interpreted
"He" to mean the God-child. There was no need for Balthazar to
suggest the importance of the dream. His two friends were able to
see this for themselves. Both princes were delighted to have received word from their friend and brother prince.

Prince Caspar in Spain had begun to pay closer attention to
the stars. Strange things were happening in the heavens, he was
told by the astrologers. There might be a mysterious omen taking
shape. Some of the stars seemed to be moving into such a formation as could lead to a tremendous crash in the heavens. Caspar
foresaw what he felt was the coming of earthquakes, floods, and
fires upon the world. If only Melchior were with him, he thought,
he could be more certain of his calculations. Nevertheless he
rested in the confidence that if there were to be any plan of action,
it would somehow be determined by Balthazar.

Caspar had liked Balthazar from the very first day they met.
He knew, when he looked at this dark, brown-black African
prince, that here was a special leader of men, unlike anyone he

had ever known or heard about. Caspar wanted him as a personal friend and was pleased when this came about. If only Balthazar could be there with him now!

As Caspar thought about these things, he remembered what Balthazar had told him when they parted. Why should he not take his charts and findings and return to the university and discuss them with Philo, his teacher? The wise old Philo would be more than willing to help. In times of difficult searching, Philo could be counted upon to come up with some answers, or else more far-reaching questions. He would go to Philo. Having made this decision, Caspar sent two messenger homing pigeons to his two princely friends to let them know, and then set off for Cádiz.

In Britain, Prince Melchior was busy meeting with the seers and magicians in his father's court. There had been days and nights of reading bones, leaves, stones, and the entrails of dead animals trying to find answers to the questions the blond-haired, blue-eyed prince was asking. The magicians also looked for omens in the sky and in the weather. Melchior fancied himself a kind of magician who had been self-made. He knew how to read his own dreams, and at times he could guess the thoughts and behavior of others. It pleased him to get messages from Balthazar and Caspar. Strangely enough, when Balthazar's message had arrived, he had felt an uneasy foreboding in his heart that he could not explain. He had wondered if his black friend was truly all right. In a dream at the time, he had envisioned a black eagle falling perilously through the sky. He knew the cause of the fall to be an evil spell cast upon the eagle by a deathly enchanter. He knew inside himself that the great bird was of royal birth.

One day when one of his friends asked why he was troubled, Melchior answered, "I somehow feel that my black friend Prince Balthazar is in trouble of some kind." The longer he remained at the castle, the more uneasy he felt. For all the wrong reasons he shrugged off these feelings and went back to looking for a kind of sign or something that would tell him when and where the Godchild would be born. He had wanted to tell Caspar about his disturbing dream, but he had not wanted to worry the Spanish prince during his studies with Philo.

In the meantime, at the cave where the broken-bodied Balthazar had been brought to recover, things were still happening. Clitus had longed for morning, but morning was yet a great way off. The angels had scarcely finished their most beautiful song and transformed themselves into creatures as high as mountains, when the earth where Clitus and Balthazar stood began to shake. The whole of the cave-temple seemed to sway back and forth, back and forth, as though some mighty hand was rocking it. From the top of the throne great drops of blood mixed with fire appeared to fall. The angels cried again with their six different voices, "Holy, Holy, Holy, Lord God of hosts, heaven and earth are full of thy glory." Thick, vaporous smoke billowed up from the floor, rose quickly and swirled around the throne. The red angel with his multicolored wings flew down from the height of the glistening stalactites at the cave ceiling. He came to rest on top of the altar, which had appeared with the magical smoke. A heap of live, burning coals glowed on that altar. With bare hands the angel lifted one and flew swiftly over to Balthazar and rubbed it on his lips and forehead. It burned and seared his face with stabbing pains, blistering his once smooth features. The blue angel descended, following the red one, and also touched his lips and face, cooling them with some oiled honey mixed with cool blue-white ice. The gold angel stood directly in front of him and said, "Now you are clean. Your sins are all forgiven. You have been made clean by the fire of the one true God, and by the honeyed ice of his love."

Balthazar fell under the weight of this revelation. The black angel flew behind him and held him up by supporting him under the arms. "You are God's man," the angel whispered in his ear. The white angel poured holy incensed oil on his head so that it dripped down his face, and said, "The blessing of the one true God is upon you." Finally, the green angel spoke: "Listen, for God Almighty himself shall speak to you."

Once again Balthazar's heart leaped into his mouth. His eyes dropped to the ground. He did not dare look up. To look at God would mean instant death. The King of all the heavens and the whole earth was ready to speak. With a voice that black Prince Balthazar felt through all his being, shaking him to the very depths, the Lord spoke: "To whom shall I reveal my secret? The whole world, its peoples, and all of creation have been waiting. Whom shall I send as my messenger? Who will go for me to proclaim the Christ? My child, my only Son, is ready to be born." There followed a silence in which the sun and moon appeared together and became pitch black while the stars wept. "Will you go for me, Balthazar?"

The prince fell forward on his face. He spoke down into the earth of the throne room. His body tensed and strained. His voice sounded like a whisper. "Here I am, Lord. Send me. Lord, send me!"

Immediately the cave was dark. Balthazar was lying on the earth floor. The only light that shone was from the flickering torches on the wall. Gone was the throne room and the throne itself. Gone were wheels, angels, smoke, fire, and altar. Gone was the beauty of it all. Clitus, no longer frozen with fear, looked down at his master lying on the cave floor. The prince was unconscious. The wound in his left side had begun to bleed. Clitus jumped up from where he lay and ran to the outer room of the cave to get the doctor. The white-bearded doctor, who had slept through all that had happened, came running as fast as his old legs could carry him. He dropped to the ground and let his half-bald head fall on Balthazar's broad chest. He could barely hear a heartbeat.

"Is he dead?" the nervous Clitus asked.

"How did he get there on the floor?" the doctor shouted. "You were supposed to keep watch over him."

"I must have dozed off, sir." Clitus was afraid to tell of the dreamlike vision.

"Help me get him back up on the bed," the doctor ordered. The two men had to strain to lift the heavy Balthazar back to the couch. Clitus held the torches close as the doctor examined the patient. "It looks very bad, very bad." The physician, shaking his head, added, "I don't know, I don't know."

The doctor did not realize that during the vision Balthazar had spoken. Once again he was forced to dress the wound in the young man's side. This time he attached leeches, with the hope that they could draw out the infection and hasten the healing.

34

The peace and quiet of the cave was ideal for the sleeping, sick young man. Clitus and the doctor took turns watching him.

On the morning of the third day after the vision, for the first time the prince stirred. His movements were accompanied by sighs and moans. Then he gasped as if trying to take in a lot of air at one time, and finally he opened his eyes. He did not see the doctor or his servant at first. Balthazar thought he was still in the throne room. Only Clitus heard the first words he uttered. "Here I am, Lord. Send me. Lord, send me."

The doctor had another servant quickly prepare some broth. Without a word, Clitus left to take the good word to the king. The prince would soon be returned to the kingdom.

Meanwhile, Melchior, still fighting the nagging feeling that things were not going well with Balthazar, decided to take matters into his own hands. With his father's permission he gathered two dozen of his best British soldiers and started off for the African city of Har'lem to see Balthazar for himself. Since Spain was not far out of his way, it would be only natural for him to stop there and bring Caspar and Philo along. Deep within himself he knew that the beginning of their mission was growing near. He felt it was time for them to share their findings with one another. By messenger homing pigeon he sent word to both Caspar and Balthazar advising them of his plans. He directed Caspar to take Philo to his father's court and await his arrival. Since it would take about two months to get to Caspar's home and then a little over three months to get to Balthazar's palace, Melchior could continue his studies and thinking along the way without being interrupted. He was convinced that their best work would be done together. Naturally Philo had to be included in their plans, since his ideas would be invaluable to them all.

Traveling to Britain's coastline, Melchior and his men boarded a Viking ship and set sail for the south. In three days' time they were shipwrecked. Half of the men lost their lives, and the survivors had to return to their villages on foot. It was at least two weeks before Melchior could start out again. This time he thought to go overland, crossing only the great Channel. It would be a safer journey with a shorter distance by sea. The experience of the shipwreck made him feel that a strange force was working against him. Perhaps it was the same force that had caused the royal black eagle of his dream to fall. This, however, made him more determined.

Once through Gaul and into the north of Spain he had to turn back again. The countryside was bedded down with the plague. People were dying like flies in summer. Again he lost half his men. He had been wise enough to carry messenger homing pigeons with him. One of these he sent to his father, ordering another ship. This one was to be built in Britain. Melchior would sail out from the west coast, plotting a southwesterly route to Spain, and then sail due east to Las Luces. Three months were required to build the ordered ship, and another month was needed to test it in the water. Meanwhile a crew was being gathered to sail her. In the end Melchior's ship was the best that had been built in the modern world up to that time.

Finally the day for sailing came, and although they faced strong opposing winds and many storms, the boat proved to be seaworthy. One time they almost capsized, but the captain, who was a Nubian slave, was able to keep the boat upright.

Melchior was tireless in his studies. He continually read his charts, studied the stars, and searched his dreams. The feeling that he was doing the right thing never left his heart or mind. In the absence of his two friends his respect and admiration for them grew. He realized how much he loved them both. One afternoon, as the ship rounded the coast of Gaul, a strong evil wind struck with fierce gusts. Melchior, who was on deck, felt stinging winds bite his face and neck. The great ship shuddered as though she was about to break up. For three hours the angry battle of the ship and Melchior against the strong evil wind continued. Finally the good winds subdued the evil gale and swept it out across the sea as mysteriously as it had appeared. Again the thought of his dream, the royal black eagle, and Balthazar burned in Melchior's mind. Something was wrong. He did not know how he knew it, he simply knew. This made him more anxious to get to Caspar and go on to Har'lem. No form of evil could stop him from joining Balthazar. The days dragged on endlessly, and the nights moved forward with a crawl. In all of this Melchior did not forget to meditate or pray. He prayed that the black prince would not have succumbed to the dark forces.

The days it took to round the western coastlines and to arrive at Las Luces in Spain seemed like years. Fortunately the waters were peaceful and calm. Friendly skies smiled on Melchior's every effort and made life worth living once again. In the depths of his soul he felt the presence of the one true God. This steadied his faith that somehow the mission that he and his two friends were embarking upon was holy, deep, and reverent. It would somehow be a mission that would finally benefit the entire world. Melchior felt that he was the most fortunate man alive.

Caspar had been anxiously waiting for Melchior's arrival. Several times a week he would go down to the wharf and the docks to see if the boat had come in. He would ask the captains of other ships if they had seen Melchior's vessel. The Spanish prince had been uneasy ever since he had gotten the news that the British prince was on his way. In the meantime, Caspar had kept himself and Philo busy trying to discover what the gathering together of so many stars might mean. He was embarrassed to remember that once he thought it would mean the end of the world. Then he and Philo laughed. The world could not come to an end until the prophecy about the God-child had been fulfilled. And maybe that very thing itself was the clue they had been looking for. Perhaps the stars were indeed lining themselves up as a heavenly announcement of the coming of the Prince of the Everlasting Kingdom. In their talks and discussions with other astrologers and their students, no one seemed to know any more than they. Actually, the others were very fearful of what the star cluster might mean.

"There is yet one thing we might do," old Philo told Caspar one evening as they sat in a tavern near the wharf.

"What is that?" the handsome young Spaniard asked.

"We could go and find Shemhazai."

"Shemhazai?" questioned the student. "Who in the world is Shemhazai?"

"She is the most accurate living sorceress in the world."

"You mean a witch?" Caspar asked, astonished.

Philo moved uncomfortably on the wooden bench. "Well,

she's not a witch in the usual sense of the word. They say she has magical powers greater than any witch." Philo did not like the word "witch." "They also say that she is older than any other person in the world."

"And how old is that?" Caspar was interested.

"She's more than one hundred and fifty years old."

"I don't believe it," the prince stated flatly.

"I saw her once, when I was just a boy. Of course she was old then. But she foretold the fall and destruction of Jerusalem. She said that Rome would increase in power and become the strongest empire the world has ever known. Why, she even predicted the bitter years of war between Rome and the Jewish rebels."

"Philo, are you sure you haven't had too much wine?"

The older man seemed to warm to his subject. His merry eyes began to twinkle. He leaned forward, toying with the empty wine cup. "Come to think of it, I clearly remember her saying that Rome had better be careful of her pride."

"Philo . . ." The prince did not finish, because the older man waved him down.

"She said a prince would be born who would not be a prince. She said he would become a king and yet never be a king. She finally said that he would die, and yet he would live."

"Sounds like a series of riddles to me." Caspar had mixed feelings about this witch. "Where does this Shemhazai live? I mean, where does she come from?"

"She lives in Sheba. Some say that she is a direct descendant of the great witch of Endor."

"And who, pray tell, was the great witch of Endor?"

"Another sorceress with great and mighty powers. It is said that for King Saul she called Samuel the prophet back from the dead so that the two men could talk."

Caspar laughed out loud. "Philo, I don't believe a word of this. It is all nonsense. I thought you might have been serious. No one can be called back from the land of the dead. No one."

"I'm only reporting what I've heard, my young lord. And you had better remember one thing that I taught you."

"What is that?"

"Not all knowledge comes from books."

Caspar smiled. He ordered more wine for himself and the old teacher. "Tell me, Philo, are you also a witch?" Caspar burst into laughter. Philo did not think he was funny at all.

At last the day of Melchior's arrival came. Caspar greeted his classmate like a long-lost brother. They embraced, jumped up and down, and slapped each other on the back. Both princes were happy to be together again. As they rode by horse-drawn chariot to the castle, Melchior spoke first of his most trying times. "It was as if devils were trying to stop me from reaching you. We went from shipwreck to many deaths by the plague. Our voyage was continually threatened. It was first one thing, then another. The very winds themselves seemed possessed. After the taunting and the discouragement, there was always the evil and wicked laughter of the winds. But tell me, what word do you have from Balthazar?"

"There has been no word," Caspar told him. "I am worried, because he always keeps in touch with us. Do you think something could have happened to him?"

"I'm not sure, Caspar, but I do know this. We must set sail for Har'lem at once," Melchior said.

"Your men should rest a few days," Caspar suggested. "The ship will need new supplies, and I'm sure there will be at least a few repairs necessary.

"Of course, you're correct as usual." Melchior agreed, but he did not like the delay.

The next day, much to the surprise of the two princes, a letter came from Balthazar. They were overjoyed to receive it. Even the king, Caspar's father, was delighted.

"What does it say?" the Spanish king asked.

"I shall read it for all to hear," Caspar said. He loosed the string that held the scroll together. After opening it, he began:

"Balthazar, Prince of Har'lem: Greetings to my friend and brother Prince Caspar. Thanks to the one true God, whom we all seek and are trying to serve, I am able to write to you. I have been quite ill of late. I suffered a bad fall. For days I lay at death's door, but the pale one refused to take me. What is more important is this. During my illness I had a dreamlike vision. This vision I wish to share with you and Melchior. You must do your best to come to me at once. I think I know what we must do. I don't know our exact path. Be sure to bring Philo with you. I am sure that old wizard will know. I am sending a like letter to Melchior. As usual we will have to wait for him to catch up with us. But we must all be together again as soon as it is humanly possible. My father the king and my mother the queen send greetings and felicitations to your most noble parents. They wish them long lives and a most happy reign. They greet you as the godson you are, my brother. Come quickly."

"So, that's why we've heard nothing," Melchior said. "Balthazar has been hurt. I have been shipwrecked. You and Philo have found only a cluster of stars and lots of superstitions. There are wicked powers working against us. They don't want the prophecy fulfilled."

"Can that be so, Philo?" Caspar asked their teacher.

"Yes, it's possible. The powers of darkness have long worked against men of goodwill."

"What can we do about it?"

"I don't know, but perhaps Shemhazai could tell us."

"Shemhazai?" Melchior almost laughed. When Caspar told him all that Philo had said about the witch, he did laugh.

"Philo!" Melchior rested a strong, ruddy hand on the older man's bony shoulder. "Nobody is a hundred and fifty years old."

Philo was adamant. "Well she is, and I've seen her."

For the next week the ship was bustling with activity. It would take yet another week to finish the repairs and the loading. Caspar, Melchior, and Philo spent much time together. They discussed their charts, findings, and opinions about the gathering cluster of stars. Occasionally they went out riding or sporting in one way or another. Melchior tried to teach Caspar the sport of free-style wrestling. Caspar thought it odd, but he soon learned its tricks and skills. They swam, practiced with bow and arrows, and tried to match each other in rope-climbing and sword fighting. They stayed up late at night and studied the stars and their various formations. Although Philo did not join them for their sports, he was always present at their discussions. Often they

40

talked so long and so late that the wise old man simply fell asleep. The young princes were beginning to know the heavens like the backs of their own hands. For a while they thought that the stars behaved in very much the same way human beings did. Each star seemed to have a personality of its own. It would be born, grow up, and sometimes seem to die. Many of these things they did not understand.

It was in the seventh month after Balthazar's cave dream, or vision, that the two princes and their teacher set out for Har'lem. Balthazar was more than pleased to know that his comrades were on the way. He had now been recovered from his wounds for four months. He had told no one about the dream-vision and had forbidden Clitus to do so. To others who knew him, a change seemed to have come over him. He was more subdued, yet he moved among people with a greater ease and quiet, radiating authority. The greatest display of emotion or energy from Balthazar came on the day a rider arrived from one of the lookout points on the great river to report the sighting of Melchior's ship. Wasting no time, the black prince with a small group of soldier comrades rode down to the harbor to meet his friends. The reunion was a joyous one.

Once at the palace, his friends bathed, changed their garments and were received by the king and the queen. After a feast in the great hall of the palace, they quickly retired to Balthazar's apartment for the planning of strategy.

"We must waste no time," the black prince said, taking the lead. "About a year has passed since this whole idea came to us. The stars are not waiting and time is not waiting."

"That much is true," Melchior agreed. Then he told them his fears about the gathering of the cluster of stars.

"What do you think such a cluster might mean?" Balthazar asked him.

"It is a definite sign of something unusual and perhaps even great."

Caspar told them what he had learned about the myth of the Egyptian god-man Osiris, and how nothing had come of it. "My other personal efforts have been frustrating," he told them. "Except for what Philo and I read in the Hebrew writings, there is not too much to go on. I have searched every source."

At this point in the conversation, Balthazar told them about his ride, the fall, and the subsequent dream-vision. He painted every vivid detail for them, so that they felt they were there. They all, including Philo, hung on every word. When he had finished there was silence, for no one knew what to do or say.

"We must do something," Balthazar said, breaking the silence. "Perhaps we can find a clue in the stars."

"Yes," agreed Melchior, "but what kind of clue?"

"Since these stars look as if they're gathering in the east, it should mean that something important is going to take place in the east."

"Whatever and wherever it is, it all has to do with the birth of the Christ-child." Melchior used the term for the first time.

After a few moments of silence Caspar spoke. "The strange thing to me is this: Why should Balthazar have his dream, and we our conviction, since we are not Hebrews? If the prophecy comes through the Hebrew writings, why then are not the Hebrews concerned for the coming of this God-child? After all, they are the one people who believe strongly in the one God."

"Perhaps they are too close to the event to see it clearly," old Philo told them. "Many times it takes an outsider to show you what is valuable in your own house."

"Well, we won't find the answer here in Har'lem," Balthazar said. "I have received my orders from the Lord God. It is now up to me and you, all of us, to find a way to carry these out."

Everyone was quiet once again. They felt that as a group they were up against an invisible wall that would not and could not be penetrated. Philo looked at Melchior and Caspar. The teacher fidgeted in his chair. He avoided Balthazar's eyes. Finally the British prince spoke. "Philo has a wild idea, but it may be better than nothing."

"What is it?" the African asked.

At this point the Greek teacher told Balthazar about the sorceress, Shemhazai. He told him everything he had told Caspar. The three princes listened attentively to every word. Although Caspar and Melchior remained skeptical, Balthazar was impressed. For a short time he said nothing. When he spoke there

42

was no doubt in the minds of the others that here was a new Balthazar. "There is no question about this. We must go to Sheba and find this Shemhazai."

"But Sheba is many weeks' journey from here," Caspar protested. "What if Philo is wrong and this whole venture turns out to be a delusion?"

"What if he is correct, and she can tell us what we need to know?" Melchior was less skeptical after hearing the story from Philo's own lips.

"We must leave for Sheba at once," Balthazar told them, coming to his feet. He strode from the room to find Clitus. Once he found his servant-friend, orders were given to make things ready. He returned to their council chamber with a smile on his face.

"All will be ready at the break of day. Dear Melchior, we shall be traveling through much desert sand. This will be too long a journey to ride horses. Therefore my princely brother . . ."

Caspar laughingly helped Balthazar finish the sentence. "We will have to travel by camel."

Melchior winced at the thought. Camels were weird and unpredictable creatures for him. One had to climb up on a camel while it was kneeling. When it got up, it rose on its hind legs first. This would cause the rider to tip forward. The first few times that Melchior had tried it, he had fallen head over heels into the sand and the others had laughed at him. Once the camel was up on its hind legs, then it got up on the front ones. All of this was bad enough, but when the animal walked it did not have the grace and charm of a horse. Its gait was a lumbering, clumsy gait that shook the body not only to and fro, but round and round, all at the same time. The British prince did not look forward to the trip at all.

During most of the night, Clitus and the other servants loaded the camels. Besides the camels the princes would ride, others were needed to carry food, provisions, and tents. There was a group of soldiers who would ward off any bandits along the way.

"Exactly where is Sheba?" Melchior asked Philo as he and the teacher readied themselves for bed in a guest room.

"Sheba is far to the east of Har'lem."

"But how far is that, Philo? You know how I love camels.

After three days on the awkward beast I can hardly walk."

"I think it's more than a thousand miles."

"And we cannot ride horses?"

"There's little water along the route. There are very few oases, and we cannot carry enough water to keep horses alive, if we ride them. The saddle of a camel is perfectly comfortable if you set your mind to it."

"My mind will never be set to it." Melchior groaned, turning over to get whatever sleep he could before daybreak.

iv

DAYBREAK CAME EVEN EARLIER THAN MELCHIOR HAD EXPECTED.
The courtyard of the palace was teeming with camels and men.
The three princes were dressed to look more like Bedouin merchants than royalty. The soldiers were disguised as traders, shep-
herds, and general travelers who were accompanying this caravan
for the purposes of safety. A few of the soldiers looked like the
warriors they were. The early-morning breeze was cool and dry,
yet it caused colorful robes and headcloths to flap against lithe
bodies.

Balthazar embraced his father and mother and strode down
the palace steps into the courtyard, where Clitus waited with his
camel. Caspar and Melchior did likewise, adding a courteous bow
to their good-bys.

"Look after him," the king whispered to the two princely
comrades.

"Have no fear," Melchior told them.

"We'll bring him back safely," Caspar said.

"May the one true God be your guide and shield," the king
called after them.

The princes mounted their camels as their servant boys held
them. The awkward, sleepy, long-necked beasts of the desert
stumbled to their upright positions, were turned by their riders,

and in two columns began to lope off toward the outskirts of the city of Har'lem on their way to Sheba. They had not gone one hundred yards when Melchior's stomach began to speak to him. He did not like what it was saying. By keeping outside of the city they were able to advance to the main caravan route and avoid the early-morning press of other merchants, schoolboys, travelers, worshipers, and city dwellers. The morale of the group as a whole was high. The hearts of the three princes were crammed with hope and expectation. Caspar, however, kept thinking to himself, There is no one who is a hundred and fifty years old.

By midmorning the sun had risen high enough in the sky to begin to make it warm. Some of the riders shed their outer robes, trying to make themselves more comfortable. The farther out they traveled, the hotter it would get. When it came to the heat of the day, or between two and four o'clock in the afternoon, they would be well into the desert and heat would do strange things to the landscape, creating the illusion of pools of water where there was really only sky and endless stretches of sand. However, there would be no water until they came to an oasis. And by Clitus' reckoning, they would not come to one for a full five days.

Sometimes in the afternoon they would pass a caravan going in the direction from which they had come. The leaders might pause long enough to ask questions or to pass along newsworthy pieces of information. Then the signal was given and the journey would continue. In anticipation of night, a suitable safe place was sought to make camp for cooking and eating supper. There they would rest and sleep for the night. The animals were tied in a safe place and usually a guard was posted to watch so that none would wander off or be taken away by night thieves.

The sun was blazing hot during the day, and the sands were very cold by night. Once in a while the party would meet blistering, wicked sandstorms that would stop them dead in their tracks. The blowing wind and pelting sand would be so fierce that the riders would have to dismount and seek refuge behind their animals. This was one of the very few times when Melchior could appreciate a camel. The contrast of a stormy day was the cool, calm night. On one such peaceful evening, the travelers sat by a campfire. The vast expanse of the blue-black sky overwhelmed the men, giving peace to their tired spirits and weary bodies.

"How many stars are there, Philo?" Caspar asked.

"No one knows," the philosopher answered. "Someone tried to count them once, but found that he could not. Someone else said that there are as many stars as there are sands of the desert."

"Who made the stars?" Melchior asked.

"I'm not sure," Philo said. "My theory is that the God or gods that made our world made the stars also."

"But could one God do all of that?" Caspar asked.

"Why not?" Balthazar questioned in return. "If he could make the world and the people in it; if he could make the mountains, the lakes, and the seas; if he could make the desert, wind, fire, and rain; if the lightning and the thunder are his, why could he not also make the stars?"

"It is too much to understand," Caspar exclaimed.

"Who needs a God he can understand?" Balthazar asked.

"But we still don't know, do we?" Caspar insisted.

"I don't think we have to know," Balthazar continued. "All we have to know is that he is somewhere up there or out there and that he desires to make contact with us. Can you imagine that somehow he wants us, you and me, to have a part in sending his son into the world? Every time I think of that I feel that my heart wants to burst wide open."

"It would be easier if we could have been there with you, Balthazar, and seen your vision," Caspar told him.

"You will see even greater things, my brothers. My heart tells me so. We three are going to be the most fortunate men who ever lived. We are going to see something that men down through the ages will envy us for."

And so, after weeks of desert travel, the princes and their caravan reached the borders of Sheba. The land of Sheba was an old, old land made famous by King Solomon, King David's son. According to rumor, David's son Solomon and the Queen of Sheba had had an intense romantic affair. She was reputed to have been one of the most beautiful women of her time. These things had happened long before Balthazar, Caspar, and Melchior arrived. Sheba was a beautiful, peaceful land, warm and friendly. Everywhere grew dates, figs, pomegranates, and good things to eat. Sheba was also an important trade center. Many caravans stopped there to sell or exchange their wares in the marketplace. The streets were filled with people and sidewalk shops selling every kind of goods imaginable. Many of the small shops burned sweet-smelling incense, and many sold trinkets of gold, silver, and bronze. Most of the people there were black or brown like Balthazar. The small children stopped to look, point, and laugh at Melchior with his eyes of blue and hair of gold.

"How do we find this witch of yours, Philo?" Caspar asked as they were walking through the busy marketplace.

"Shhhhh." The old teacher held a skinny finger up to his lips. "The streets here have ears. Everything and anything that is said here goes right to the ears of Shemhazai. It is said that she knows everything."

"I still have the feeling that we've come this long way for nothing," Caspar told the others. "Remember I've never believed in this witch from the very start."

"I am thirsty and would like some cool coconut milk," Balthazar told his companions. "See, over there—that looks like an inn. Perhaps we can get something to drink there."

They made their way through the press of the crowds and entered the inn and sat down. Soon a young man came and asked what they wanted. Balthazar ordered some coconut milk for the four of them. Caspar and Melchior also ordered some fruit to eat. They ate in silence, for Balthazar appeared to be deep in thought. They were baffled, for Philo did not seem to know what to do. Presently another young boy approached them and bowed in reverence.

"Which of you is the noble Philo?" he asked.

The startled old teacher nearly choked on his drink. He bolted upright. "Why, I am!"

"You are to come with me."

"Where is he to go?" Caspar asked.

"I cannot say that. I am told that he must come with me, and he alone."

"Who is sending for me?" the old man sputtered.

"One who knows all about you. You will not be kept very

long. You three princes are to wait here."

The boy spoke with authority. Balthazar immediately felt that Philo should obey him. When the others got up to follow, he restrained them. A smile grew slowly upon his calm and handsome face.

"Where do you suppose he's going?" Melchior asked. "And why did you let him go?"

"The lad called us princes," Balthazar told them. "How could he have known, since we do not know anyone here?"

Melchior's eyes opened wide with astonishment. "That's right, we don't know anyone here."

"But someone here knows us," Balthazar said. "We are to remain right here until Philo comes back. When he does, we'll learn what we need to know."

In silence they waited for Philo. One hour turned into two, and two hours into three. Caspar was very definitely worried. Melchior was ill at ease, but Balthazar was the picture of self-contentment. He sat calmly with his eyes closed as if he was praying or meditating. A few moments into the fourth hour Philo came back into the inn. He was out of breath.

"Where in the world have you been?" Melchior asked.

Before Philo could answer, Balthazar spoke. "He's been to see Shemhazai."

"Shemhazai?" questioned the other two princes.

"Yes," answered the surprised Philo, "I have."

"But how did you know, Balthazar?" the others asked.

"Remember, I pointed out to you that the young boy called us princes."

"Yes," answered Melchior and Caspar.

"I also reminded you that we are strangers in Sheba, and that no one knows we are princes. We have come here in disguise."

"Very clever deduction, Balthazar. I have taught you well," Philo said.

"What did she say?" Caspar was still confused.

"As we came into the city we passed an old deserted temple," Philo continued.

"I remember it," Melchior said.

"We are to be there this night of the new moon, and we must

be there at the witching hour. She will meet us and tell us all we need to know."

"Does she know why we've come?" Balthazar asked.

"She said she will tell all. And, Caspar, she told me to tell you that the charm you bear around your neck marks you as your father's choice to succeed him to the throne."

Caspar gasped in amazement, because in his land succession to the crown did not necessarily pass to the oldest son.

"Well," Balthazar said quietly, "maybe now you'll see whether or not Shemhazai is what Philo claims that she is."

For the rest of the evening they decided to go out and mingle with the people. At the marketplace they listened and laughed at the storytellers. They ate at an inn different from the one where they had stopped for the coconut milk. Townspeople began drifting off to their homes, while strangers and travelers sought shelter in the various inns. The streets were not safe against robbers and wicked men at night, even in Sheba. At yet a third, smaller, and more friendly tavern, the three princes found themselves drinking warm wine, working up courage for their midnight visit to the old temple. Caspar and Melchior wanted to ask Philo more questions about what had happened during his absence.

"How long will it take us to get to this place?" Melchior asked.

"About half an hour from the city gates," Philo told them.

"Did she seem friendly?" Caspar touched the charm around his neck.

"Most friendly," was the answer. "But more than that, she told me quite a few things I wanted to know."

"Did she say anything about the stars?" Caspar asked.

"You'll know in due time." The old philosopher smiled.

"How long do you suppose we'll have to stay in Sheba?" Melchior asked.

"I hope we'll stay for a little while, at least," Balthazar said. "I'd like to get a good look at this place, since we have not been here before."

"You seem terribly calm about this whole thing," said Caspar.

"I am, my friends, I am."

The princes did not know that the old ruined temple where

Shemhazai had decided to meet them was in reality the very palace that had belonged to the Queen of Sheba. At the stroke of midnight the four of them were there. The deserted place had a gloomy look about it, for there was no roof. There remained only the outer walls, and parts of walls that once separated various rooms. The men gathered in what had been the main great hall. They made a fire because the night air was colder than they could bear. The flames cast ghostly shadows upon the old, decaying walls. Shadows danced before them, stimulating their imaginations. The warmth of the fire came to them, and, as they grew more accustomed to their surroundings, an eerie light began to appear gradually in the great hall. The light, with its accompanying particles, looked as though it was beginning to turn in a counterclockwise circular motion. The princes could not be sure, but there seemed also to be some kind of moving about within the light itself. This movement within the light became more solid, until human shape and form began to emerge. Melchior and Caspar became frightened. Even though they had heard of ghosts and spirits, they had never thought they would live to see any. Balthazar, though curious, was not afraid. The light grew brighter and stronger, and the human form became clearer. Although the form was surely a woman, it never quite stopped shimmering.

"Welcome to the three princes," said the voice. It sounded like someone speaking from behind the light.

"We are grateful that you have come to us," Balthazar said, since he was the only one who could speak.

"You have come to me as a part of your great mission. I put it into the mind of Philo to bring you here to seek me."

"Are you as old as Philo said you were?" Caspar blurted out.

"I am even older," said the woman. "I am a direct descendant of the witch of Endor. But do not be deceived by the name 'witch,' for I am a spirit of good fortune."

"Then you know why we have sought you," Balthazar said to her.

"You are brave, the three of you. You are chosen by the Great Spirit who governs the heavens, the earth, and the universe." The three princes remained silent. The voice continued, "Your mission is not going to be an easy one. There are other forces that would stop you. However, at all costs you must go out and seek the God-child, for unless he is found and proclaimed to the world, his coming will have been in vain."

"Then the child is to be born?" Balthazar asked.

"The child will be born very, very soon. And you, Balthazar, it is you who will know and recognize him. Without your proclamation, all else will be for nothing."

"But why me?"

"Because you have sought for him with all your heart. I know of what happened to you in your cave after your great fall. That fall was meant to kill you. The Great Spirit, however, sent his angels to guide and protect you, to keep you from falling into the jaws of death."

"How shall we know the child?" Melchior asked.

"You shall know him because you have been studying the stars. The stars will tell you."

"But the stars look as if they are going to crash and there will be great calamity upon the earth."

"That is not so, my prince. The stars are coming together in order to announce the birth of this God-child. If mankind did not proclaim it, the very heavens themselves would cry out."

"Why then is it so important for us to find him?"

"Because men are foolish. They only believe what other men will tell them, what other men have seen."

"Where will we find this child?" Philo asked.

"You shall find this child where the sun rises."

"And where is that?" Melchior asked.

"In the land of the wicked king," Shemhazai answered.

"What was your original prophecy about him?" Balthazar asked, wanting to get the information clear in his own mind.

"A hundred years ago, I foretold that one who was a prince would be born, but he would not be born like a prince. He would be a king, yet the world would not receive him as a king. Finally, he would die, yet out of that death would come life."

"But what does that mean?" Caspar asked.

"There are some things I must leave you to discover for yourselves."

"Please tell us how we shall know him," Melchior asked.

"I can tell you only this: Balthazar will hold the key to his discovery."

"Are there any further instructions, Shemhazai?" Philo asked.

"Yes, you must leave Sheba tonight. Go back to Har'lem and there assemble a new and larger caravan. Be sure to take soldiers with you, for there will be perils along the way. Remember that you are going to find a king. Therefore be prepared as you would be in visiting any earthly king. The stars will be a clue for you.

"If you remain pure in your hearts and in your thoughts, you shall find what you seek. You must also beware of those who pretend to be your friends. They are the ones who are most dishonest."

"We thank you, O great one," Balthazar said to her.

"One final word of warning, Balthazar. You must be careful of your wound. If it is opened again, you will surely die. Do you understand me?"

"Yes, O great mistress."

"You have my blessing and my protection, as much as I am able to give. Now go in peace and be on the alert. The forces of darkness do not want the child to live, or to be found."

The three princes and their caravan left for Har'lem that very night. The joy and anticipation of finding the God-child helped the weeks of travel to fly very quickly.

When they arrived at Har'lem, Balthazar immediately sought to speak with his father. The two men talked alone, because Balthazar knew that whatever he requested would be a great risk to the king, in spite of the fact that he was assured of his father's trust. They talked far into the night. Melchior and Caspar wanted to return to their homes in order that they might better prepare themselves, but Balthazar would not hear of it. He believed what Shemhazai had told him—that time was of the essence, and that they would have to move quickly.

It took several days to organize this new caravan. Fortunately Melchior and Caspar had brought a goodly number of men with them, so that they each had fifty trusted soldiers. Balthazar had fifty, but left it to Clitus to recruit a hundred more.

"We cannot be too safe," he said, reminding the other two of

Shemhazai's warning. "We do not know what lies ahead. Therefore we should be prepared for anything."

"I think we should rehearse the men in mock battle," Caspar said.

"You have just found yourself a job," Balthazar told him. "Include my men in your practice as well. Every man must be able to use his sword, shield, and small knife. He should be able to ride, use the bow, jump, climb, and be swift in self-defense."

"Are you expecting trouble, Balthazar?" the noble Melchior asked.

"I am expecting anything and everything," Balthazar replied.

"Do not be unmindful of your wound," Philo warned him.

"I have been thinking about that," Melchior told them. "So while you all have been planning the strategy of battle, I have had a special girdle made that should protect Balthazar from any usual kind of wound. It is made of iron mesh."

"It will take some sword to penetrate that," Caspar told them all, looking at the protective armor. "By the way, Melchior, I shall need your help in training the men."

"And I shall see to the provisions and materials we shall need for the journey," Balthazar told them.

"But, do we yet know where we are going?" Melchior asked.

"Philo, suppose you tell them," Balthazar suggested.

The old teacher scratched his bald head and began to speak. "Young prince Balthazar and I have taken your calculations about the formation of the stars and added to it what we were told by Shemhazai. It is our opinion that we shall have to travel toward the east. We're going to have to go into a land of Semites, the country of the Hebrews."

"That means Herod's country," Melchior said. "I've heard of him from my father. He is supposed to be so sly that he is called the Old Fox."

"My father says he isn't to be trusted," Balthazar added. "Go on, Philo."

"If you will remember," said Philo to the three young men, "in our earlier talks we decided that the Hebrew scriptures spoke about the coming of a king. Where Herod rules is now the center of the world. It is reasonable to suppose that the child will be born somewhere near there. After all, we must remember that Shemhazai said we were to travel eastward. If you will recall your charts, the cluster of the star formations that we have been watching for almost two years now is gathering in the east. So our guess is that this is the general direction we must seek."

"There are several other things we must do." Balthazar came to his feet. "We must not tell our men, except for our personal servants, where we are going or why. There must be no leak of our mission. Remember that Shemhazai said that there are those who would do the child harm. No one outside our inner circle must know our mission."

"All right, so we leave, and so we travel to the east. Yet how in the world will we find him?" This was Melchior's question.

"Shemhazai said we would know. She said that I would recognize him. I don't know what that means as yet, but I think it will come to me as we go along," said Balthazar.

"Finally we must remember that there are astrologers and sorcerers at the court of Herod. Perhaps they will know something that will add to our knowledge. But under no circumstances must we ever let any outsider know the true reason for our traveling. In fact, I have a message from my father to Herod, as well as chests full of gold and precious gifts, so there will be little reason for anyone to suspect that our presence is anything more than a state visit."

"When do we leave?" Caspar was anxious to begin.

"Not until we solve another riddle," Balthazar replied. "It has to do with the true purpose of our journey. We are going to visit a much greater king than Herod. By this I mean the child who is soon to be born."

"Why then should we not begin our journey at once?" Philo asked.

"I'm surprised, dear teacher, that even you do not know," Balthazar said. He turned to Caspar. "Caspar, dear brother, suppose for a moment that you were king in your father's stead, and I was king in mine. Suppose I sent an ambassador to your court, what would you expect from him?"

"Warm greetings, of course, a message, and some knowledge of your personal health," replied his friend.

"But what else would you expect?"

"What else would there be?" the Spanish prince asked.

"A gift!" Melchior bellowed. "Every king expects a gift from any other king, no matter how friendly."

"Exactly," said Balthazar. "We are not only seeking a child, but we are going as princes to pay homage to a king. And this we know, my brothers, is no ordinary king."

"Then we can't take ordinary gifts," Caspar suggested.

"True, but neither can our gifts be so great that they draw attention to us or to him," Balthazar reminded his friend.

"What then shall our gifts be?" Melchior asked.

"I'm going back to my cave," Balthazar said, "to the cave where I had the vision. You must carry on here without me. Clitus will complete the gathering of provisions. I need to meditate and pray. I'm sure Shemhazai has given us the clues that we need, but I'm not sure what they all mean."

"How long will you be gone?" Caspar asked.

"As long as is necessary. But you will have things to do here. We must be sure we have enough provisions to last us a long time. We do not know how long we will be gone or when or how we shall be coming back. Caspar and Melchior, my father has written to your fathers explaining to them very carefully the nature of this expedition and all that it involves. He has requested some talents of gold and silver to help with the expenses. We shall not wait for them to arrive, for my father believes in what we are about to do. We shall go forth in full confidence and faith that we shall not fail in what we have been chosen to do."

Balthazar left for his cave, and the others busied themselves with the training and the readying of the men. Philo stayed close to his charts and began to read signs and omens wherever he could find them. Balthazar's father kept no magician or sorcerer at his court, so from time to time the king and the teacher had interesting talks. When everything was ready, in addition to the two hundred and fifty soldiers and their provisions, there were sixty camels, thirty-five donkeys, twenty-five horses, and two personal servant-bodyguards for each of the princes. Balthazar's father watched all these preparations with great pride. He knew in his own heart that he could not stand in the way of the son whom he loved.

In the cave, Balthazar prayed and meditated. He almost hoped that he could relive that most glorious vision once again, but that was to no avail. Except for the occasional blowing of the wind, or a torch giving off sparks, there was no sound. He became aware that someone or something was blocking him, so that he could not find the wisdom he sought in order to guide the caravan safely.

v

"O Lord God, enthroned above the wheels and the six colored angels, I feel that we are now ready to embark upon this important mission to which you have appointed us. I am grateful for comrades like Caspar and Melchior and our teacher, the wise Philo. Keep us from danger and harm. Grant us courage and wisdom to know what to do and when to do it. We don't know everything, and without you it is so easy for us to fail. I am here seeking a final clue as to how we can come to find and know that part of you which is going to become man by way of a newborn child. May we be steadfast and alert. Keep us from selfishness that would get in the way of our success. Evermore do we seek your favor and grace. . . ."

Balthazar paused in his prayer. He felt the silence echoing in his ears. Bowing his face toward the ground in the direction where, in his dream, he had seen the throne, he whispered the phrase "Here I am, Lord. Send me." Although he did not go into a trance or fall asleep, an idea began to dawn upon him. He remembered Shemhazai's riddle and thought that perhaps he now knew what kind of gifts he and the others might take along. The trip could be postponed no longer. They would have a good night of sleep and start off with their men at daybreak.

He returned to the palace. After they had eaten supper, the three princes sat in the council chamber with the king and Clitus.

"What did you decide?" Melchior asked.

"If others are already seeking to destroy this child, even before he is born, we must be careful," Balthazar told them.

"We have already agreed on that," Philo said.

"During my meditation I thought about the clues that Shemhazai gave us. She said that he would be a prince, but he would not be born like a prince. That would of course mean that he would not be born in a palace, nor would he necessarily be rich."

"That makes sense," Caspar said. "Why didn't we think of that?"

"That means we'll have to take him a gift of gold!" Melchior clapped his hands.

"Gold, yes," Balthazar said, "but not too much of it. Not enough to make people suspicious. Just enough to let it be known that we recognize his royalty."

"What else did you discover?" asked Philo, almost jumping up and down with excitement.

"She said he would be a king without a kingdom. That means that his influence certainly shall grow, and perhaps not too many people will know or recognize him," Balthazar replied.

"Maybe it will be better if he is not recognized," Caspar said.

"I don't know whether that is true or not, but if he is a king, or to be a king, he will undoubtedly have a kingdom of some kind. Therefore, it seems to me another gift is in order."

"Cloths of purple and fine linen?" Caspar asked.

"No," Balthazar said, "I thought of that, but it would give him away to his enemies, especially if he is not to be born in a palace. It would make jealous princes suspicious and might even place him in danger. Besides, expensive cloths of purple and fine linen do not make for royalty."

"What makes for royalty, then?" Melchior asked.

"A man's bearing and the way he carries himself," Balthazar answered. "My forefathers could have told you that. They were captives and slaves, not permitted to dress in royal robes, yet the

60

enemies of Carthage always treated them with respect. No, clothes do not make the king.''

"Then what does, or what will?'' Philo was impatient.

Balthazar answered, "It must be something symbolic. I suggest frankincense, because it is such a rare essence and fragrance. It lasts and lasts. It is used only by royalty.''

"It is also not conspicuous in the way it looks,'' Caspar said. "I shall make that my gift. When the child uses it from time to time it will remind him of his own royalty until he can assume his kingdom.''

"And what of the third part of the prophecy?'' asked Philo in deep reflection.

Balthazar's features darkened. "He is to die, yet is to live again. The only gift I can think of for a dying king is the gift of myrrh. It was used in the burial tombs of the ancient pharaohs, whom the Egyptians thought were gods. Perhaps myrrh is the right gift. If and when he must die—notice I say 'if,' because I'm not too sure what Shemhazai meant by this—the myrrh will make him know that he is royalty and that life eternal is his.''

"You actually believe that he will die and live again?'' Caspar asked.

"I don't know what I believe about that. But I do think that these three gifts are as meaningful as we can make them. I do not pretend to understand it all. After all, Shemhazai spoke to us in the form of a riddle, and these gifts offer symbolic meaning and perhaps an answer. I think that we have chosen well.''

The king said nothing but smiled. In that moment he was proud to have a son like Balthazar. He also knew that if anything should happen to him, with his son the kingdom would be in good, safe hands.

"My best judgment says that Balthazar is correct,'' Philo added. "After all, we were told that it would be he who would recognize and proclaim this God-child.''

Daybreak brought with it the shout of a journey's beginning. Captains shouted to their men. Overseers ordered groups and squads into action. Horses whinnied and neighed. Donkeys brayed under their loads. Camels chewed their cuds and lumbered carelessly forward. The three princes and their servant-bodyguards led the whole company. The king and the queen stood out on the balcony watching the caravan parade by. The air was filled with joy and anticipation. For once this was a great expedition in the cause of peace and love, and not for war. The sun blazed like a crown of orange-red glory in the sky. The heavens were clear blue with the promise of success. The whole of the countryside was hushed and still, as if participating in what was beginning, and hoping for what would come.

The caravan would have to move slightly northward for a while and then dip down toward the south in the direction of the Red Sea. From time to time, Caspar would look behind and see the following of so many men and feel content. At least for the time being, with that number, they would be safe from bandits.

Since they were crossing a large, vast desert, every day looked like every other day. There was nothing but sand and sky, sky and sand. Occasionally, off in the distance, they saw vultures flying about where some poor creature had died in a vain attempt to cross that almost endless expanse of sand. The heat was so great that always on the horizon there were the infamous devil lakes. When caravans arrived at these points, they would find nothing there but sands. Much to their relief, the travelers were escaping the fury of sandstorms. The weather seemed to favor them wherever they went. Following a route mapped out for them by Philo and Clitus, they reckoned themselves to be making excellent time. They arrived at their first oasis right on schedule. Here they were able to rest and water the animals and take stock of their provisions. They could also attend to the personal needs of their men before moving on.

The pleasant, carefree journey could not last long, for all the time they had been planning, practicing, and packing for it, evil eyes had been watching them. When Melchior and Caspar had first arrived in Har'lem, this was great news, because of their royal rank. Everyone was curious, including those who wished them well and those who sought personal gain through evil designs. Among the latter of these was the old desert bandit chieftain known as Nebuchadnezzar.

Nebuchadnezzar kept spies in Har'lem because of the many caravans going to the east, south, and north. When he heard of this one and the fact that it was being led by the three princes and a group of two hundred and fifty soldiers, he surmised that something important was happening, even though he did not know what it was. He guessed that they were going forth to meet and greet one of the eastern kings. From the size of the group he reasoned that they might be going to visit King Herod. Any visit to Herod meant gold, silver, and other precious stones. Nebuchadnezzar knew that Herod was greedy, for he was greedy himself. Therefore, all along the way, even though the princes did not know it, they were being spied upon. Nebuchadnezzar wanted to avoid an all-out attack on the caravan itself. He would lose too many men that way. If he could find out where the gold and silver was, that would be enough for him. He could steal it and take it off to his hideaway camp in the middle of the desert, known as the Valley of Magic Sands.

The journey continued uneventfully. As each day passed, the princes and the men grew more and more relaxed. When they came to the village of Malakal they decided to take a two-day rest.

"Thank heavens," Melchior said. "I am so happy to get down from that crazy beast of a camel."

"The men deserve the rest." Balthazar smiled. "We've been making good time. The animals should be freed from their burdens for a while, and also the horses should be rubbed down."

"What are your orders, my prince?" Clitus stood before Balthazar.

The prince touched his right shoulder in friendship. "We three, with you and the other bodyguards, can remain in town. The men will have to find a place to camp outside of town and erect their tents."

"I think we can leave that to the captains," Caspar suggested.

"I agree," Balthazar said. "Why don't you give the order while Melchior and I see to our lodgings. We will send Clitus to you when everything is arranged. Tonight we eat good food, drink good wine, and sleep in good, clean beds."

Melchior rubbed his backside and his legs. "I am every bit in favor of that myself. Forgive me, my brothers, but I still have no love for camels."

"But, noble prince," Clitus said, "were it not for the beast you do not like, we could not proceed on this our holy quest."

Balthazar and Melchior set about finding their sleeping quarters. Again they would maintain a disguise, passing themselves off as merchant leaders of a caravan. Each prince would take a sleeping room with one of his servant-bodyguards, and the other three guards would share a room of their own. Fortunately they found their rooms situated in such a way on the upper floor of the inn that they were connected. Casually they would eat downstairs, mingling with the other guests to throw off any suspicions as to their backgrounds or mission.

As Melchior and Balthazar saw to these things, Caspar rode out of town to where the captains had camped to make sure that everything was in order. It was important that the gold, silver, and precious jeweled gifts for Herod be well protected. Not even the captains knew about the gold, frankincense, and myrrh, which had been placed in three ordinary-looking chests. This was to keep anyone from becoming too curious. When everything had been checked to his satisfaction, Caspar sat down to collect his thoughts about the journey ahead. He was so deep in thought that he did not hear Balthazar's messenger until he had been called the third time. Then Caspar again mounted his camel and with the servant returned to the inn, where his friends were awaiting him.

"How are the horses?" asked Melchior, wishing he could ride one.

Caspar smiled. "Everything is in order, including the horses, but to ride them now is out of the question. They would use up three times as much water, and it might even kill them. No, we must save them so that when we get to Jerusalem we can make a grand entry that will impress the old fox, Herod."

"I wonder what he's really like, this Herod," Melchior said absently.

"We shall soon find out." Caspar sat down at the table. "I'm hungry, and the captains have everything in order."

"Then the camp is secure?" Balthazar asked.

"As well as can be expected," Caspar replied, "but I for one would feel better if we had brought the treasures along here with us. I fear danger, but I don't know why."

"Balthazar is right," Melchior explained. "Bringing the treasure here would attract too much attention."

"It will be good to have two full days of rest," Caspar said as he poured himself a generous glass of wine.

"Just don't forget that we're supposed to be merchants," Balthazar reminded them. "Until we get to Jerusalem no one must guess who we are."

As Balthazar spoke these words, someone did know who they were. The bandit Nebuchadnezzar had been following the caravan from a distance where he could not be seen. He knew every trail and route that caravans or lone travelers might take. Unknown to the three princes he was not too far from their inn. In his tent in the hidden Valley of Magic Sands he was striding up and down, listening to the report of two of the spies he had planted in Balthazar's caravan.

"So, you had no trouble getting into the troops of the black Balthazar?"

"No, Nebuchadnezzar," one of the spies said. "When we heard that he was looking for men for a long journey, we knew something important was going to happen."

"And what have you to report?"

"We're not sure where we're going," said the second spy, "but we do know it has something to do with Jerusalem and Herod's court. We are taking a lot of gold, silver, precious cloths, and jewels to Herod."

"So, gold, silver, and other precious things," the desert chieftain mused, stroking his black beard. "You are sure of this?"

"Yes, Nebuchadnezzar, you would not believe that the three princes have disguised themselves as merchants and are staying in the village. The treasure is in the camp with only a small group of men to guard it."

Nebuchadnezzar laughed evilly. "That will make things easier for us. So they are without leaders in camp! How many days will they remain in this camp?"

"Tonight and tomorrow night," the first spy told him.

"Well, if the leaders are posing as merchants, we too shall do so. First we'll have a closer look at them in town, then we'll ride out to that camp tomorrow afternoon and make off with the treasures."

"But they have so many men, how shall we be able to do it?"

"I have a plan all ready," said Nebuchadnezzar. "You go back to camp and leave everything to me. The only thing is this: you must learn and know exactly where the treasure is, so that when our men come for it they can take it by surprise and with ease. I shall see to it that you are not followed or molested."

The spies had not told Nebuchadnezzar everything, for they did not know about the three small chests carrying the real treasure for the real king.

That evening things proceeded normally. No one had reason to be on guard. The captains released more of the men to come into the village, since there had been no sign of danger. The inn where the men gathered was noisy in a friendly way. Nebuchadnezzar slipped into town in disguise so that he might have a closer look at the three so-called merchants. Although he did not speak to them, he observed them closely. There was no doubt in his mind that they were more than merchants. They had a difficult time disguising their courtly manners. Nebuchadnezzar acted so cleverly that no one discovered who or what he was. The evening passed leaving everyone in a cheerful mood.

The sun rose bright and early the next morning. Very rapidly the temperature changed from warm to hot. The princes and their servants slept well. It was Caspar who volunteered to ride out to the camp and inspect things. The others bathed and readied themselves for a day of leisure. They planned to go to the marketplace as soon as it opened and look for interesting things that they might take home for gifts. Philo went immediately to find the temple to question what holy men or seers he might find. He was interested in knowing whether anyone in the village studied or knew about the stars. No one yet spoke openly about the mission. Each prince seemed to know what the other was thinking. Such was the spirit of friendship and trust, that there was no need for words. The journey itself was drawing them all closer together.

After lunch, Melchior and Balthazar retired to their rooms to sleep. Toward the cool of the day they got up and decided to take one last look through the marketplace. Balthazar thought it best that they separate. "We should keep our eyes and ears open, in case we hear anything about the stars, or news of a strange child being born anywhere along our route."

The open marketplace carried the usual kinds of wares. There were sellers of trinkets, medals, lucky pieces, bracelets, and necklaces, which were not expensive. Some of the stalls sold carpets, draperies, and fine linens. There were of course articles of the finest silver and gold. The princes were impressed by what they saw, but bought nothing. They were mainly seeking information. Each shop had its own news, but none of it was of value to the princes and the journey. Philo had wandered into the temple and had had no luck at all. The temple wise men did not understand his language, for none of them spoke Greek or Latin as Philo and the princes did. He liked what he saw of the temple paintings and sculptures. He was even delighted by the design of the temple itself. Philo thought that places of worship often told him things about the people who worshiped there. He was reveling in his thoughts about their trip to Sheba. He was pleased that he had made a believer out of the doubting Caspar, who at first had not taken Shemhazai seriously. The one or two secrets she had shared with him would help him in his own studies and personal search. He was startled at the temple entrance when a man who looked like a warrior came up to him.

"Hail to thee, most noble Philo," the man said.

Such a greeting startled and frightened the old teacher.

"How do you know my name?" Philo asked.

"Nebuchadnezzar has ways of knowing a lot of things."

At the sound of that name, Philo became terribly disturbed. His mind raced ahead to many possibilities.

"Do you recognize this charm?" he was asked as the bandit showed him a royal signet charm.

"I do." Philo whispered because he was apprehensive, knowing at once that it belonged to Caspar. Philo had spent more time with Caspar than with the others.

"You will take this charm and this message to the black Prince Balthazar. Tell him if he wants to see Prince Caspar alive again, he must obey every detail of this letter."

With that the bandit was gone. Philo gathered his robes around him and ran down the temple steps, heading back for the

67

inn as fast as his small legs could carry him. Even before he arrived at the inn's gate, he was yelling for Balthazar and Melchior. Only Clitus was there.

"What in the world is the matter with you?" Balthazar's servant asked him.

"Where is the prince?" Philo gasped for breath. "Where is he? Something terrible has happened."

"He is at the marketplace with the royal Prince Melchior," the black servant answered.

"We must find them in a hurry! In a hurry, do you hear! Go, fetch them and tell them to return here as fast as they can."

Clitus found Melchior before locating Balthazar. The three of them returned with haste to the inn. There they found Philo pacing up and down nervously.

"What's wrong, Philo? Ants in your robe?" Melchior questioned.

"This is wrong," Philo answered, thrusting the charm and the note into Balthazar's hand. The black prince looked at the charm and read the note. He handed it to Melchior.

"They've got Caspar. What shall we do?"

"Exactly what the note says," Balthazar replied. "If we go out to the camp, they will kill him. If we don't, they will set him free."

"You mean you hope they will," Philo said. "Nebuchadnezzar is the most powerful desert bandit chief in all of North Africa."

"He says that we must not go near the camp until nightfall. We will do what he says. He also promises that Caspar will be released by the time the moon rises tonight. That will be during the second watch. We will wait."

"But what of the treasure and what we have set out to do?" Melchior asked. "The mission is no good without the treasure."

Balthazar looked at his British brother. "Look, it is obvious that the treasure is what Nebuchadnezzar is after. If we try to rescue Caspar now, we may lose him and the treasure as well."

"Then we cannot make a move, can we?"

"We can follow the instructions as given. Once Caspar is back and safe in our hands, we'll know what to do."

In accord with the information of his spies, when Nebuchadnezzar and his men raided the camp there were no leaders and only a few soldiers to guard the treasure. The others had gone into the village, eager to make merry because of the long trip that lay before them. Finding the treasure intended for Herod's court was easy. Nebuchadnezzar was surveying it hungrily when one of his henchmen dragged in a tied but undefeated Caspar.

"What have we here?" asked the desert bandit chief.

Caspar pulled and tugged at the arms that held him in an iron grip. He tried with great effort to wrench himself free.

"We found him in one of the smaller tents with these," said one of the desert chieftain's men, pointing toward the three smaller chests brought in by three other bandits. Caspar still tried to free himself. He pulled two of his captors off balance, but they fell into him and knocked him down.

"We will have an end to your trying to escape," Nebuchadnezzar told him. "You will yet prove to be a valuable hostage."

"Your best plan would be to leave this camp as you found it, Nebuchadnezzar. If my two friends get their hands on you . . ."

"Pardon the interruption. It is not if they get their hands on me, it is if they ever get their hands on you, my dear Prince Caspar." Nebuchadnezzar turned to his henchmen. "Take him to the Valley, and make sure he is well hidden and not permitted to mix with the other hostages."

"Yes, Nebuchadnezzar."

Caspar pulled and pushed, but was wrestled and dragged from the tent, for there were too many for him to fight, since his hands were tied behind his back.

"Well, now, what is this?" The bandit chief opened one of the small treasure chests. The fragrance of frankincense rushed at his nostrils. "Ah," he thought, "I can get a very pretty penny for that." When the second box was opened he saw the myrrh. He did not know exactly what that was for, but felt it must be worth something to be carried in the special chest. At the opening of the third box, he jumped up and down for joy, because there was nothing in it but purest gold. All this was much more than he had bargained for. He chuckled to himself, "So, they were posing as merchants, eh? I'll bet there's plenty more where all of this comes from." He stroked his black beard once again. "This is the very best loot I have captured in years." The desert air echoed with his devilish laugh. Caspar turned in the direction of the sound as he was being forced upon a horse to be taken away.

Balthazar and Melchior, along with Clitus and Philo, sat nervously through the first watch, waiting with apprehension for the second. The moments seemed to drag past. In the dreaded silence, they all realized that now the entire trip and its purpose were in mortal danger. Balthazar refused to think about going on without Caspar. He reasoned that if by some miracle Caspar did escape, the treasure would be in the hands of Nebuchadnezzar, and no one knew where to find that desert jackal. The thought that they might have to begin all over again tore at his soul. There won't be enough time, Balthazar thought, without saying it. We'll never find the God-child if we have to start all over again. He did not trust Nebuchadnezzar, and so when Caspar had not returned by the second watch, he was not surprised, but was angry instead.

"What do we do now?" Melchior asked his comrade, for he too was angry.

"There is nothing we can do tonight. At the break of day we'll ride out to the camp and see if we can pick up a trail of some kind."

"Following a trail in the desert will be difficult," Melchior told him. "The wind blows over the sands quietly, leaving no tracks. I don't see how we can find him or the treasure."

"You don't see, and I don't see. But my friend Clitus here, what a gift he has for tracking! He can track even the wind."

The wound in Balthazar's side began to hurt. At that moment he forgot that he was only an earthly prince with simple, earthly problems. The pain reminded him that he was a special man with a calling, and the success of that calling depended upon his being where he had to be, when he had to be there. Shemhazai had warned him to be careful. He thought he had been, but evidently he had not been careful enough. What should he do now? He knew that Melchior would be right.

When they rode out to the camp the following morning to see what damage had been done, the men were in disarray. Those who had been there when Nebuchadnezzar came told of how he ransacked the entire camp. Luckily no one was killed. Balthazar ordered Melchior to regroup the men. He told Clitus to scout around to see what could be found of the bandits' trail. He and Philo would go back to the village and see if they could find a trace of the desert chief. Perhaps some of the village merchants knew something and would volunteer the information. Balthazar was very angry. In a sense he feared for his own life, for the wound was increasing in pain and he did not want it to open.

Their daylong search in the village was futile. They questioned everyone with whom they had had contact. Those who knew about Nebuchadnezzar were too frightened to tell anything to the angered black prince. He even offered gold for information, yet no one came forward. Angrily he and Philo left the inn and went out into the night. Clitus had very little to report. He had picked up a trail but had lost it several times.

"I am going to the temple," the black prince told Philo and Clitus. "I want you to wait for me in the outer court. I am sure there must be an answer to all of this and I am going to find it."

Balthazar entered the temple. It was not unlike the temple in his own city of Har'lem. There was a marked difference, however: this temple had idols. Nonetheless it was a peaceful place. With the light of the moon and the additional light of the wall torches, one could see reasonably well. For a moment, the prince did not know what to do. Then he saw an altar with the inscription on it, "To the Unknown God." His heart pounded loudly in his chest. He did not know the full meaning of the inscription, but at least it carried the suggestion that this Unknown God might be the same one true God he and his comrades had been continually discussing with Philo. He knelt in silence before that altar, upon which there seemed to burn an eternal flame. It was almost as if the fire had a life of its own. It seemed to be full of wonder and spirit. He stared at it for a while. The longer he looked at the flame, the more it reminded him of his original experience in the cave-temple. The fire even began to take on six different colors as the angels had done. Finally, miraculously, it took on the form of a woman and reminded him very much of the seemingly ageless Shemhazai. He prayed:

"I am here, O Lord, sent by you on your mission. What is it that I must do? I must find Caspar and save the treasure or I shall never find your divine child. Without your help I can hope for nothing. The sands of the desert have swallowed up the bandit's trail. I must find Caspar and rescue him. May no harm come to him. Give to Melchior and me the strength to do that which we must do."

His ears began to tingle. From the light and heat of the flame there seemed to come a musical sound. Within that sweet sound there were words. Balthazar could not tell whether the voice was male or female.

"You must return to the inn. It will be told you there what you must do. Again I warn you, be careful of your side. The wound must not be opened or you shall surely die."

The colors of the fire all at once blended into one, and the altar was as Balthazar first saw it. He was satisfied, however, that he had gotten what he came for. He left the inner court of the temple and found a shivering Philo and an alert Clitus waiting for him. Philo had been dancing up and down with the cold. When he heard they were returning to the inn, he was glad, even though he did not know what this had to do with finding Caspar and the possible recapture of the treasure.

vi

PHILO HAD NEVER SEEN BALTHAZAR WALK SO RAPIDLY AS ON THEIR
return trip to the inn. The teacher was pleased to get immediately
into bed beneath the warm covers. He had had a very full day.
Very quickly he went to sleep.

Balthazar, Melchior, and Clitus sat quietly in their shared
room, brooding over the events of the day. Each was quietly keeping his own counsel. The tension created by the waiting was unbearable. Balthazar could read the frustration in Melchior's blue
eyes. They both loved Caspar and they both were silently praying
for him. Time moved on and they sought to fight the tiredness
that was trying to overtake them. Would the mission fail? What
would they say to Balthazar's father concerning the stolen treasure? What would they say to Caspar's father if he did not return?
Just as the three men began to nod, there came a quiet, timid
knock on the door. Clitus was first on his feet. He crept stealthily
to the door. Looking at Balthazar, he waited for the signal. The
black prince drew his sword, Melchior his knife, and Clitus saw
Balthazar's head bend forward slightly. The door jerked open,
and to everyone's surprise there fell into Clitus' strong arms one
of the servant girls who worked in the inn downstairs, helping
with meals.

"I'm sorry to disturb you, great sirs," she stammered. Melchior laughed uncontrollably as the girl was quaking with fear.

Balthazar was embarrassed at the drawn weapons. He signaled for them to be lowered. "What is it that you want?" he asked gently. "And who are you?"

"I am the maid Eunice. I work here at the inn." She looked down at the floor, not daring to look into the eyes of the handsome prince. "You have been asking for the whereabouts of Nebuchadnezzar."

"Come in, quickly," Balthazar said gently, pulling her inside. "What do you know about this bandit chieftain?"

"I know that he has been holding my father prisoner for many years. I know that everyone is afraid of him, and that even the Roman soldiers have been unable to find him."

"Why have you come to us?" Melchior asked.

"I've heard that you wish to find out where he is—where his hideaway is, I mean. I know where it is. I know how to get there."

"Can you tell us how to get there?" Balthazar was becoming excited.

"I can tell you, but you would never find it. It is not called the Valley of Magic Sands for nothing."

"Can you take us there? I shall reward you with whatever you want," he promised.

"I should only like to have the freedom of my father and those of his friends who are kept there by the cruel Nebuchadnezzar. They act as his servants and slaves."

"Show us the way to the Valley of Magic Sands, and I shall personally guarantee your father's freedom," Balthazar told her.

With the speed of lightning, Melchior awoke a disgruntled Philo. The teacher complained sleepily that he had just begun to have a good, warm dream when he was so rudely disturbed. His reprimands, directed at no one in particular and everyone in general, continued until they were in the barn behind the inn, saddling the horses. The four of them, with the girl Eunice, made their way from the inn and village out to where the camp had been reconstructed. Balthazar shouted orders to Clitus, who in turn shouted them to the captains. The soldiers were roused out of their sleep and found themselves having to get ready for battle. Horses had to be saddled, armor had to be put on. Shields, knives, and swords had to be made ready. The night air was electric with excitement. Once everything was ready they were set to go.

"Pass the word along," Balthazar told his men. "We must go silently. There must be no noise. We want to surprise this devilish Nebuchadnezzar and make him sorry for the very day he was born."

The trail led out across the moonlit desert. The sands themselves cast curious shadows in the night. The wind blew silently as if giving its consent to the coming events. The stars twinkled with joy in anticipation of Balthazar's success in finding the hidden valley.

"Why is it called the Valley of Magic Sands?" he asked Eunice the maid, who rode on his horse with him.

"There is nothing like it in the whole desert world," she told him. "It is actually an entrance into a secret cave, behind which is a hidden valley. It cannot be seen even when one is near it, because the sands continue to fall like water before its opening."

"You mean like a waterfall?" Melchior asked.

"Exactly like a waterfall, except it is sand."

"But how can it keep doing that forever?" Philo was fully awake.

"In this area of the desert there are many sandstorms. When such a storm comes it replenishes the supply of sand that is lost during the times of peace and quiet. Many men have looked for this place and have not been able to find it."

"How did you find it?" Balthazar asked her.

"Many of Nebuchadnezzar's men come to the inn. Of course some of them get drunk and talk. Once I took it upon myself to follow them until I knew how to get to this place by myself. I have been praying day and night that someone would come along and help me rescue my father and his friends who have been longtime prisoners there."

"How many men do you think the old vulture's got in there?" Melchior asked.

"Some think he has close to three hundred men. Many of them are fugitives from Roman colonies or other places. Most of them are cutthroats, thieves, and murderers."

"About three hundred, you say?" Balthazar smiled. "With our

two hundred and fifty, that should make things very interesting. Wouldn't you say so, Melchior?"

"Quite interesting. I wish they had more so the sides would be more even."

The rest of the ride was in silence. The night wore on and became darkest just before the skies began to break into a predawn gray. The rays of the morning sun could be seen stretching toward the vault of the heavens. It was going to be a good day. Suddenly, for a moment, a wave of cold fear swept over Balthazar. In his eagerness he had forgotten to put on the mesh girdle of iron that would protect him in close fighting. It was too late now to go back for it.

At last they reached the entrance to the Valley of Magic Sands. As the girl had said, one could ride directly past it and never see it. The falling of the sand continually hid the entrance. That much Balthazar thought was good, for at least their arrival would be unsuspected, as no strangers had ever entered through the sand falls. Once inside, Balthazar and his men quietly shook the fallen sand from their garments. Strategically he led his men in such a way as to form a large ring around the whole camp of Nebuchadnezzar. Much of the camp was asleep. Down below he saw a tent, where he counted a group of five guards. They appeared to be special, for all other sentries around the camp were separated by distances of at least a hundred and fifty yards. Clitus took account of them and was already issuing orders to have them taken care of.

Balthazar surmised that Caspar must be in the tent with the five guards. His blood began to warm as a prelude to the coming battle. He whispered to Clitus, "Do you think you and two other men can get down there and silence those guards?"

"Your wish is my command, O great prince," said the servant.

Clitus selected two other trusted soldiers and began to make his way quietly down the sides of the embankment toward the tent. It was yet early morning and although the five guards were supposed to be on duty, two of them were asleep. Clitus crept up behind one guard and covered his mouth as he stuck his knife into the soft flesh of the bandit's back. The two other hand-picked soldiers strangled the flank guards. The two that were asleep were knocked on the head to make them unconscious and they were

76

tied up. All this happened in a matter of moments. Balthazar watched silently from where he sat on his horse. Presently he saw Caspar emerge. Balthazar and Melchior waved vigorously but made no noise. Caspar made his way up the ridge and embraced his comrades.

"Where are the other prisoners kept?" Balthazar asked.

"They are in that compound beyond the far ridge."

"Can you get there and free them?"

"I shall need about twenty men. That compound is well guarded, but once we set the prisoners free, that should even up the numbers."

"We'll give you time to get down there. When you've broken through, give a shout and the rest of us will swoop down on old Nebuchadnezzar. He won't know what hit him."

Caspar took his men and began to creep down the slope. The sun continued to climb in the sky. Balthazar and Melchior hoped that they would have enough time to profit from the element of surprise. Just as Caspar had gotten half way, one of the guards who had been knocked unconscious woke up and managed to work himself free. With a shout and a yell he ran toward the main tent where Nebuchadnezzar slept, waving his arms and shouting a warning. Balthazar realized at that moment that he and his men could not wait for Caspar, so with a great roar they galloped down the side of the hill and into the valley itself. Swords were drawn, shields were raised, horses were guided downward, and the two sides met. Nebuchadnezzar's men came streaming out of their tents with swords, shields, and knives in their hands.

The two forces came together with clashing fury. The noise of steel against steel echoed in the morning air. Horses stumbled and fell. Some of them landed on top of their riders. Other riders were leaped upon by Nebuchadnezzar's men and thrown to the ground. Some soldiers lost their swords and had to fight with their bare hands or with their shields. Others jumped to the ground as quickly as they could and caught some of the bandits off guard, not giving them a chance to get their weapons. There were cries of struggle, pain, anguish, fear, and even death. One of Balthazar's men was the first to fall. In the meantime, Caspar had reached the compound. He found it more difficult than he thought it would be to break through. The guards there had already been alerted. The fight at the gate was fierce, for the bandits were all waiting for him. Again swords were drawn. Sparks flew from the crash of metal against metal. Many of the men simply fought with their hands. Bodies were thrown into the air and down onto the ground. Caspar's comrades fought hard and well. Shouts and screams echoed from ridge to ridge. Caspar, advancing on the compound, fought like a tiger. Melchior, moving in the direction of archers and horsemen, fought like a bear. Balthazar, taking on foot soldiers and javelin throwers, moved with the grace of a leopard. Wherever their swords slashed, men fell to the ground. Although they were outnumbered, their will to win gave them the extra force they needed to beat the enemy down. Nearing a heavy wooden gate reinforced with iron and pitch, which had been put up to keep the prisoners more secure, Caspar cut the locked heavy chain in two, and the prisoners inside rushed out like a flood of dammed-up water to come to his aid.

Balthazar and Melchior continued advancing. Philo found himself a corner and sat nervously counting bodies and figuring the chances for Balthazar's victory. The battle raged on for one hour, and then two. As the third hour began, it was evident that Nebuchadnezzar's forces were tiring. Many of their men had been wounded or killed, and others were doing their very best to escape. Balthazar was not troubled with those who were trying to escape. He was determined not to let the evil old bandit chief get out of his sight. He finally fought his way into the chieftain's tent. When he entered he saw immediately the chest of jewels that had been intended for Herod, as well as the other chests of gold, silver, and costly gifts. He did not see the small chests of the gifts that had been prepared for the God-child in the name of his companions and himself.

From the shadows, Nebuchadnezzar rushed at the black prince like a madman. His sword, held high, came down in a chopping blow aimed to strike Balthazar a fatal blow on the head. The black prince dodged out of the way just in time and drew his own sword. The bandit chief was skilled with his weapon; he had had years and years of practice. He lunged at the black prince. He thrust, he swung the blade around and executed some very clever deceiving blows. Balthazar had all he could do to keep out of the way. He knew that if the chieftain could kill him, he would. Nonetheless, the black prince showed his own training. He too was skilled with that weapon. He handled it as though it were a part of his own hand and body. The sword seemed to obey his every wish and will. He was able to keep Nebuchadnezzar at a healthy distance.

But Balthazar fell over some crates and Nebuchadnezzar was on top of him. He lunged with his sword, but missed. Balthazar rolled out of the way, but in coming to his feet he dropped his sword. The bandit chief backed Balthazar away from his sword to keep the advantage. He rushed at the black prince, who quickly grabbed a hanging curtain and used it as a lash against the deadly sword of his enemy. For a few moments he was able to keep Nebuchadnezzar at bay.

Finally Balthazar had no recourse except to pull his knife. But what match was a knife against a sword? It was evident now that Nebuchadnezzar was going to move in for the kill. He was a greedy man. He had seen the gold, silver, precious jewels, and fine linens. He knew what was in the three small chests, and he was not going to let them slip through his fingers. He jumped at Balthazar, who moved to one side and then to the other. With his back to the center pole of the tent for support he waited as Nebuchadnezzar came at him with the fury of a desert sandstorm. Balthazar ducked and the sword of his attacker chopped at the wood of the tent pole, sending chips flying off in every direction. Nebuchadnezzar quickly recovered a sense of balance and thrust forward angrily. Balthazar felt a stinging, hot, sharp pain, but only for a brief second. The force of Nebuchadnezzar's thrust was so great he did not see the poised knife in the prince's hand. He fell upon that knife, letting out a groan and yell. Blood rushed forth from his mouth. His eyes rolled back into his head. He fell backward, and in a moment he was dead.

The tumult of battle died down on the outside. Melchior and Caspar had managed to put the rest of the bandits to flight. The servant girl, Eunice, could now move freely into the camp, where she saw her father and tearfully embraced him. The sight of the two together pleased the three weary comrades. The rest of the prisoners were happy and pleased once again to be free men. Shouts of victory and freedom spread through the camp. It was not until noon that peace and quiet reigned and Balthazar could speak.

"You need never worry about Nebuchadnezzar again," he told the cheering men they had rescued. "You are now all free men. You may return to your homes and your families."

"We are grateful to you, O great prince," said the servant girl's father.

"And what is your name, sire?" Balthazar asked with respect.

"I am called Paulus. I am king of Media, not too far from here. Nebuchadnezzar was holding me hostage until my people could raise the gold and silver necessary to ransom me. We are a poor people and that could not be done."

"You are a freed man, King Paulus," Balthazar said, "and except for what was taken from us by Nebuchadnezzar, my comrades and I would think that you are entitled to all of his spoils." Balthazar looked around at Caspar and Melchior and they smilingly agreed.

"Is it all right with you if I claim this land and make it part of my kingdom?"

"It is a beautiful spot," Melchior mused. "Since you have suffered so much and your people have been robbed even of their freedom, we think you should claim it."

"So be it then," said Paulus, who was very happy to be reunited with his daughter. "I shall this very day set things in order. I'll leave one of my princes in charge here, and on the morrow I'll ride out to my people so they may see me once more."

"Remember our kindness to you," Caspar said to him. "Rule your kingdom with kindness and justice for everyone, and we shall not be sorry that we have helped you."

"This I solemnly promise," King Paulus told them.

Later the three princes gathered in what had been Nebuchadnezzar's tent. The treasures were still intact, making the loading of them very easy.

"There is one matter we have not yet solved," Balthazar told them. "Our own special treasures are still missing."

"You mean the gold, frankincense, and myrrh?" Philo asked.

"Yes, I have not been able to find them here in the tent," said the black prince.

"Nebuchadnezzar hid the chests in a special place," Caspar told them.

"Do you know where?" Balthazar asked.

"No, I don't. I was brought here and put into the compound before he got around to doing anything about it," Caspar told them. "I've been asking, but no one seems to know anything."

The three princes were baffled, Not even the offer of one hundred talents of gold could help them find where their special treasure was hidden. Even though they had rescued Caspar, restored King Paulus to his people, rid the desert of Nebuchadnezzar, and found the treasured gifts for Herod, they were still downcast.

"We cannot leave until we find those gifts," Balthazar cried. "That is the key to everything."

Each sat in silence, thinking where the gifts might be. No one had an idea. Then, in the peace and quiet that usually follows such excitement as the battle they had fought, an amazing discovery was made.

"Balthazar!" Philo exclaimed. "Look to your side, you've been wounded!"

Through Balthazar's battle tunic a thick red substance was slowly seeping.

"My God in heaven!" exclaimed Caspar. "You've been wounded!"

Balthazar's hand brushed against the tunic. "It's nothing, just a scratch. We'd better return to the inn, where we'll be able to think more clearly."

The three princes, together with Philo and Clitus, returned to the inn after Balthazar instructed the captains about returning to their original camp outside the village of Malakal. On the ride back, Balthazar was the picture of bravery and confidence. He remembered that Nebuchadnezzar had wounded him, but in the heat of battle he had not felt the pain. Now, he was fearful. He hoped that this fear did not show on his face. Philo, who knew what Shemhazai had said, began to worry.

Once back at the inn, Balthazar asked to be left alone with

Clitus and Philo. He did not want to worry Caspar and Melchior. As he lay on the bed, Clitus carefully removed his shirt and undergarments. The skin was smooth and dark. It had an almost velvet glow to it. Nevertheless, near that fatal wound, there was a slow flow of blood. Philo looked at it closely and shook his head, his face somber.

"How bad is it?" Balthazar asked.

"I don't know," the old teacher told him. "Clitus, bring me some warmed water and some clean cloths."

The servant did as he was told. Philo fretted in silence. Balthazar tried to cheer him, but that was to no avail. Lying there on his side, he could not see the wound. As the hot cloths touched it to clear away the excess blood, he gritted his teeth. He winced but did not make a sound. Philo had Clitus bring the lamplight closer so that he might get a better look at the prince's side. The sword had punctured the skin and entered the forbidden area of the old wound. Philo slowly turned pale, for he did not know what to do. His hands trembled as he attempted to stop the flow of blood. For a few moments he seemed to be successful, but he was not sure. Again Balthazar asked the question, "How bad is it?"

"It's a clean cut," Philo managed to say.

"Is it near my other wound?" Balthazar asked.

"I'm afraid that it is." Philo did not like the sound of his own voice.

Balthazar said nothing. He remembered only that he had been warned. I must not die now, he thought, and I must not tell the others. I've got to find the gifts and I've got to find the God-child.

"You must clean the wound as best you can, and bind it tightly, Philo," Balthazar told the trembling old man.

"I shall do the best I can."

"Better still, you hold the lamp and let Clitus do it."

"Yes, yes, that is better, isn't it?"

"Clitus, I want you to bind it tightly so it will bleed as little as possible. And I forbid either of you to tell the others about this wound."

"But," Philo protested, "they have a right to know. Just in case . . . in case . . . in case anything should happen to you."

82

"They'll know when it's time for them to know." Balthazar was definite in his statement.

"You need not worry about me, my lord," Clitus told him. "I shall say nothing until you say it is all right."

"Good, and that's the way I want it."

Even though there had been a loss of blood, Balthazar did not seem weakened by it. Yet he was apprehensive, for he did not know how far the wound had been opened or how long it would be before Shemhazai's prophecy would come true. Come what may, he had to live long enough to recover their special treasure; and he had to live long enough to see and embrace the holy child. Then, he thought to himself, dying would not be such a bad thing after all.

Once the wound was dressed and covered, he left his rooms and joined the other princes downstairs in the inn. To show them he was yet in good spirits, he drank some wine with them and joined their talk.

"We still have the problem of trying to find our special gifts," Melchior reminded Balthazar.

"It is very obvious that Nebuchadnezzar hid the chests because he was not going to share the contents with his men. If that were not the case, then we would have found them with the things we were taking to Herod."

"But where would a thief hide things from other thieves?" Caspar asked.

"That's for us to find out, and we must do so quickly," Balthazar told them. "I have an idea. You two wait for me here, and perhaps we can yet solve this riddle."

He left the inn and went out into the night air. He walked in the direction of the temple. Once again before the altar of the Unknown God he paused, looking into the flame. Once again the fire danced before him. As he watched it in deep meditation, the flame, as before, changed into six distinctive colors. His whole being became transformed. He felt as if he were in his body and out of it at the same time. He dropped slowly to his knees, wanting to speak but not knowing how to start. Gradually the words formed in his mind.

"You know my heart, O Unknown God. I have begun this quest by your command. My heart is heavy, for we have lost the treasured gifts that we had prepared for your Son. In addition, I know that I am mortally wounded. I know that I shall die. But, I beg of you, O God, I plead with you, since you have chosen me, let me not die until my job is completed. I do not ask for a long life. I do not even ask to reign over my people. I only ask that you let me live until I have finished that which you have appointed me to do. I pray this desperately. Let the light of your favor and grace shine upon my comrades. Keep them in the light of your love. Bring them safely to their kingdoms once again. And, as I wait before you, stimulate my mind, so that we may quickly find the treasures we want to bring to your Son. I pray it because I trust in you. Amen."

He continued to stare at the flame until he had lost all sense of time. Once again the flame took on the form of a beautiful, divine woman. His heart leaped again for joy. He thought for a moment that he would not be able to contain it all and that he would cry out. "Fear not, Balthazar," a voice cried within him, "fear not."

At that very moment Philo came tramping noisily into the temple. He was not aware that Balthazar had been in prayer and meditation.

"Balthazar, O my prince. My brave black prince. I have figured out where the treasure must be."

"Where?" the black man asked.

"Right here in the temple. It can't be anyplace else. This is the first place a thief or a bandit would hide treasure, because he has no fear of God, the gods, or holy men. It is only other evil men in the desert he fears."

"You may be right," Balthazar said. "But where would it be?"

The thought came to both of them at the same time. They struggled to move the altar of the Unknown God, and sure enough, behind it in the hollow they found the three smaller chests. Everything in them was as it should be. Balthazar paused

84

long enough to say a great thank-you to his God in his own heart.

"Philo, you have helped to save the day. Go and get the others. I'll need help to remove these from here."

With the gifts fully recovered, the princes were once again truly happy. Balthazar said nothing about his wound, nor did Clitus, nor did Philo. On the following morning they gathered together the men who had survived the battle. Those who could travel would continue on with them. Those who were wounded would stay behind until they were well enough to return to Har'lem, where everyone would meet once again when the mission was completed. Those who had fallen in battle and had given their lives would be buried with honor at the spot where they had made their camp. Balthazar commended them all, living and dead, for what they had done. The two who had spied for Nebuchadnezzar were caught in a tavern and were hung. Later that day Balthazar and his caravan moved on toward Palestine and the city of Jerusalem, where Herod had his court. Balthazar thought it best to send two couriers ahead of the main body to let the city know that they were coming. He did not want to take Herod by surprise, for his father had warned him that this king, who still ruled by permission of the Romans, could not be trusted. Every step would have to be planned in order not to raise the suspicions of the sensitive Herod. The caravan, it would appear, was traveling solely to meet Herod at his court.

"Where are we going to stay in Jerusalem?" Melchior asked.

"Sooner or later it will be at the palace, I'm sure," Balthazar answered. "However, in the meantime, so that we can get the lay of the land to understand just what is going on, my father has given me a letter to an old friend of his. I'm sure we shall be invited to stay there."

"What is this friend's name?" Caspar asked.

"He is called Joseph of Arimathea. He also has a son of the same name about our own age, so we should get along well there. The elder Joseph has been friends with my father since their youth. He is noted for being an honest and just man."

"It will be good to be with honest and just men once more," Melchior said.

"My father tells me that the elder Joseph also believes in the one true God. So it may even be possible that he can give us information that we are seeking about the holy child and also about the stars."

The sun faced them in the mornings, stood directly over their heads at noon, and cast long shadows upon the sands in the evenings. Peace and gentleness had again returned to their caravan and their journey. The three comrades were feeling their customary fellowship with one another. Secretly, after Casper and Melchior had gone to bed, Clitus would carefully dress and tend Balthazar's wound. It seemed that the black prince was getting no better. In fact, at the end of each day there appeared to be a greater loss of blood. He did not speak about it, and he continued to forbid his servant to say anything. Philo kept reading scrolls upon scrolls, hoping to find a remedy of some kind that might be of help to the ailing prince, but there was none. How long Balthazar could hold out, none of them knew.

Jerusalem, city of David, city of peace. From as far as ten miles out, the sun could be seen reflecting from the gold that adorned the roof of the palace and its equally famous temple. Here was the city of Herod the Great, as he called himself. Jerusalem was a city of more than a million inhabitants. There were people there from every known nation under the sun. Many of them were Jews but some were not. Most of them were Roman subjects even if they were not Roman citizens. The city gleamed and glistened in the noonday sun. The three princes were relieved to be there, for somehow they felt much closer to fulfilling their purpose. Three miles from the city, couriers met them to announce that King Herod was pleased with their coming and would welcome them at his court. After they had had suitable time for a rest and a visit with Joseph of Arimathea, servants would be sent to escort them. What Herod did not say was that he did not like the elder Joseph, for he was one of the few nobles who dared to find fault with the king openly.

The home of Joseph of Arimathea was palatial in its own right. Balthazar had heard from his own father that the man was very rich, but upon seeing the household, he found it difficult to believe. It was a beautiful household where one could hardly tell the slaves from the members of the family.

"There are no slaves in this house," the old patriarch had told them. "We believe in the one God, who has made all men equal."

"Who is this one God?" Balthazar asked eagerly.

"The Jews call him Jehovah, but I am sure he is known by other names."

"It is good of you to welcome us into your home," Melchior told him.

"The pleasure is mine. I have heard of your father, Prince Melchior. His fame at conquering the barbarians has come down even to us. While all of you are here in Jerusalem, this must be your home. You must feel free to come and go as you please."

"We are grateful for your hospitality, sir," Caspar said.

That night at dinner the conversation continued. Balthazar took the lead in the discussion. Seated at the table with the princes were Joseph's wife, his daughter, and his son, the younger Joseph, as well as Clitus and Philo.

"You say you've come seeking a God-child?" the elder host asked.

"The cluster of the stars seems to be gathering in this part of the world," Philo said.

"We know about that," young Joseph said. "I, too, have been studying the stars. But here we must be very careful. They do not call Herod the Old Fox for nothing. He has spies everywhere. He does not want to hear of such an unusual child. You see, many of the Jews hope that one day the child will be a king."

Balthazar thought silently of Shemhazai's words, "He shall be a king, yet not a king." He did not say anything.

"There are rumors to the effect that such a child has already been born," the wife of Joseph said.

"Where?" asked Caspar.

"We think it may be in Judea," young Joseph volunteered, "and that is not too far from here."

"But no one here can or will go there. Herod has forbidden it."

"Why?"

"He is afraid of the news they will bring back."

"But he cannot forbid us to go there," Melchior said. "We are princes in our own right. We are not subjects of Herod."

"Besides," Balthazar said, "my father, knowing of his crafti- ness, has sent along a few expensive gifts for the old sly one. Per- haps we can simply pull it off when he sees what we've brought."

"He is rather a glutton," said the elder Joseph.

Philo stood up for a moment. The three princes and the others were startled and did not know what to say.

"Philo, what is the trouble this time?" Caspar smiled. "More ants in your tunic?"

"I'm sorry," sputtered the teacher, "but tell me, sir, do you have a scroll of the Hebrew scriptures here in the house?"

"Of course we do," said the elder Arimathea. "My son Joseph will be happy to show them to you."

"I must look up something and I must do it right now," Philo exclaimed. "You must excuse my manners."

The others around the table laughed. Balthazar winced and Clitus noticed it. He knew that his young master was bleeding again.

"We must go to Herod's court and see if we can learn any- thing," Melchior said. "I am told that, next to my father's court, Herod has more astrologers, seers, and magicians than anyone else."

"That much is true," Joseph's wife said. "When our son Jo- seph was born, one of Herod's astrologers told us that he would someday be a man of great distinction."

"I dismissed that," said the elder Joseph. "After all, I am a rich man, and when I die he will inherit everything."

"Yes," agreed his wife, "but they went on to say that beyond the fact of being rich, young Joseph would be remembered for a very heroic act."

"We've all laughed about it," continued the father, "for, as you can see, he is not a warrior like yourselves. He is rather a scholar and solely bookish. I don't know what can come of that."

The conversation around the table continued. The princes re- laxed as if they were in their own homes. The atmosphere was warm and pleasant. It was difficult to believe that outside the walls of the compound there was a cruel world, filled with cruel men, whose hearts were filled with evil and mischief.

Presently Philo returned to the table nearly running. He was literally hopping up and down. The younger Joseph returned to his seat.

"I've found it!" cried Philo. "I've found it!"

"You've found what?" everyone exclaimed.

"I've found the very thing I've been looking for. Ever since we got this idea there has been something in the back of my mind plaguing me, and I did not know what it was until you, sir, mentioned the word 'Judea.' That's the modern term for Judah."

"What has that got to do with anything?" Melchior asked.

"Just this." Philo could hardly stand still. "With young Joseph here, I searched the books of the prophets, and guess what? It was the prophet Micah who said that out of Judah would come a governor."

"Wonderful!" Caspar shared Philo's happiness.

"It's true," young Joseph exclaimed. "I read it with him as we looked it up. His Hebrew is quite good."

"But Judah is a big place, is it not?" Caspar asked.

"Not so populous as Jerusalem. It is a province with many small villages. If something is going on there, you should be able to find it out."

"We most certainly shall go there," the black prince declared. "But first we shall pay our respects to King Herod, telling him nothing, yet seeing what we can find out."

"May I come with you?" young Joseph asked.

"You certainly may," Balthazar said. "After all, you will be our guests. Herod cannot refuse you admission to the court if you are with us."

"My only words are these," said the elder Joseph. "Be very careful and very wise. Herod is so crafty he has spies that spy on spies."

That night as Philo and Clitus dressed Balthazar's wounds, they both realized that things were not getting better but were getting worse.

"I think we should tell the others about this; it's not improving," Philo said, calling Clitus aside.

"Balthazar has forbidden us to speak about it," the servant reminded him.

"He may be a prince to you as well as to me; but I am his teacher and I know that this wound is not improving. Someone had better have a look at it. We should summon a doctor."

"You will make him angry if you do so, or, if you tell anyone."

"Caspar and Melchior have a right to know," Philo insisted.

"I suggest that you wait a little while longer. I shall try to reason with him. Maybe after we have seen Herod we can persuade him to seek help here in Jerusalem. There are some excellent doctors here."

"If that does not work, then not only shall I tell the others but I shall send a message to his father, the king. Mark my word, Clitus, I have seen wounds like this before. If this one does not heal quickly, Balthazar will not live to find the God-child."

vii

HEROD'S TEMPLE WAS TRULY ONE OF THE GREAT WONDERS OF THE
ancient world. Large areas of the marble walls were overlaid with
pure gold so that they always glistened in the sun. The towering
gates were of bronze, or overlaid with gold and silver. The arcades
and courtyards where merchants sat selling sacrifices to wor-
shiping pilgrims were appealing to the eye. The merchants sold
pigeons, doves, and young lambs, all of which would be offered in
sacrifice upon a huge, impressive altar in the center of the inner
courtyard of the famous temple. Herod had replaced the older
temple with this costly and magnificent building. He wanted everyone to think of him as a deeply religious man, even if it was not
true.

Herod's palace was likewise impressive. The guards were
dressed in bright array of red and gold. They lined the walkways,
which were cradled by green trees and well-kept shrubs. There
was also a reflecting pool that lent serenity and tranquillity to the
garish splendor. It was a sight to make any monarch or prince en-
vious. The palace steps were made of marble, and it was these very
steps that the three princes ascended in their finest royal dress.
Each was followed by his personal servant and by another group
of servants carrying the presents and gifts for the devious Herod.

The court was crowded with nobles, ladies, and religious leaders. Most of them had come to get a glimpse of Balthazar, for the fact that he had killed the notorious Nebuchadnezzar was already known to everyone. In addition, Herod had never before entertained a black prince who was destined to become king of a domain larger than his own. Servant girls walked before the princes and threw flowers into the air for them to walk upon. Trumpets heralded their arrival, and an honor guard of Herod's own personal force was there to bid them welcome. Balthazar insisted upon walking with the young Joseph of Arimathea at his side. If this unnerved Herod in any way, the crafty monarch did not show it. A young servant stood by and announced the visitors to Herod.

"His Royal Highness Prince Caspar, Prince of the Spaniards, and heir to the throne of Spain." The process of greeting was repeated.

"His Royal Highness, Balthazar, Prince of Har'lem, and its next king," he proclaimed. Balthazar stepped forward and bowed slightly before Herod. The ladies of the court were straining their necks to get a look at this handsome young black man. Herod merely nodded his head in acknowledgment, while toying with the black curls of his beard.

"His Royal Highness, Prince Melchior, Prince of all the Britons, and next in line to be their king." Vocal "oh's" and "ah's" could be heard as the court strained to look at Melchior, for his golden hair and beard, coupled with his blue eyes, made him a curious spectacle. King Herod bowed slightly in approval and acknowledgment of his guests.

"Welcome to Jerusalem," Herod said to them. "Long may your fathers reign. Our court is honored by your royal presence."

"Greetings to you, O great Herod," Balthazar replied. "The whole world has heard of your greatness and your mighty deeds." He continued, "Behold, we bring you greetings from our fathers and have brought gifts for you, your royal Majesty."

Herod nervously pulled at his beard. He did not want to appear too anxious, but he was very pleased to hear about the gifts. The chests were brought forth and opened. When Herod saw the gold and silver, the rubies and sapphires, his heart beat for joy. It was the final gift that overwhelmed him. Balthazar had also brought along a heavy chain pendant made of flashing emerald caught in a pure gold net. The hue of the stone was the deepest, purest green the great king had ever seen. Immediately he put it around his neck.

"As long as you remain in Jerusalem," he said, "my kingdom is at your disposal."

"We thank you for your graciousness," Caspar told him.

"You must be my guests here in the palace for a few days," Herod insisted. He was not unaware that the princes had come with another purpose in mind. He was determined to find out that purpose. "In fact," Herod added, "you have come at a good time. My youngest daughter is betrothed to a nobleman's son, and we are giving a great party and banquet in their honor on the evening of the morrow. In the meantime you shall have every comfort."

"We do not mean to impose upon your graciousness, your Highness," Melchior began, "but we have been guests in the home of the honorable Joseph of Arimathea. It would please us to have him present with us at the banquet."

"And to have his son remain here with us as our companion," Caspar added hastily.

Herod squirmed uneasily for a few moments, looking at each of the young men. He stared at his well-kept hands, fondled the emerald pendant, and then smiled. "Of course, you shall have your request," he told them.

The princes were shown their lavish living quarters, and young Joseph of Arimathea accompanied them. Herod had servants appointed to see to their personal needs, but there was no doubt in the princes' minds that these servants were spies. It was difficult for the three friends to meet, to talk, and to plan.

"If the child is to be born in Judea, or is already born there, why hasn't Herod been told about it? Why doesn't he seem to know anything about it?" Caspar asked.

"It is obvious that he does not want to know," Philo said. "He's not about to share his kingdom with anyone else."

"Philo," Joseph said, "you and I must try to get together with the court astrologers and magicians. We know they are among the best. We must see what we can find out."

"If that fails," Balthazar said, "we'll have to risk telling the Old Fox the truth."

"If the child is to be a king, that could place him in danger," Caspar reminded them.

"That's a chance we'll have to take," Balthazar said. "I'm not too sure that he will want this kingdom anyway."

"Why do you say that?" young Joseph questioned.

"I'm not sure," Balthazar told him. Then he related the experience they had had with Shemhazai. "You see, if he's to be a king and yet not a king, then his kingdom must not be like this one. It appears to me that a son of God, or child of God, would not be limited to one kingdom."

"You mean he might be king of the world?" Joseph asked.

Balthazar snapped his fingers. "I think that might just be it. Of course, that must be it. God would be terribly selfish to send his son just to be king of one people or one nation. If God is the God of us all, then his son must be king of us all."

"King of Kings," Philo said absently.

Immediately Balthazar's mind went back to his vision. Simultaneously his side began to hurt and bleed. Hurriedly he left the room, calling for Clitus and Philo to follow him.

"What do you suppose is wrong with him?" Melchior asked.

"He's keeping something from us," Caspar said. "I've been watching him since he fought with Nebuchadnezzar. There are times when he is simply not himself."

"Maybe he needs our help."

"Let's not push him yet," Caspar suggested. "I know Balthazar. He doesn't like people to pry into his affairs. He would resent our intrusion. We'll give him a little more time."

Later that day, while the princes and their servants strolled through the royal gardens, Philo and young Joseph of Arimathea met with the court magicians and astrologers.

"We have noticed the star cluster you have spoken about," the chief astrologer told them. "When we mentioned it to his Majesty, he dismissed us both. He said that his kingdom shall last forever and that he is not concerned for what the stars seem to say."

"What did you think they meant?" Philo questioned.

"At first we thought some great disaster was about to come upon us. But then we changed our minds. The magicians threw their bones and sticks and said that it meant some great event was about to take place, but we did not know where. We still don't know."

"In fact," one of the magicians whispered, "we have been forbidden to speak about such things."

"Don't you have any theories?" young Joseph questioned. "You must have. My father has been concerned about these things."

"I should not tell you this," the first astrologer said, "but I have known your father for a long time. He has a very devout friend whose name is Simeon. My advice is for you to seek him out. Perhaps he can tell you more. He is not afraid of Herod, for he is considered a holy man."

That evening while changing for dinner, Melchior heard a knock on his door. He was surprised to find Herod's son standing there.

"Excuse the interruption, Prince Melchior, but I wanted a word with you privately."

"But of course, your Highness," Melchior said.

"Of all the princes, you are the most interesting. We never see men with yellow hair in this part of the world, and of course your eyes of blue make you almost magical."

"You flatter me, young prince."

"I know why you're here," young Herod said. The room suddenly became still.

"I'm not sure what you mean," Melchior said, continuing to dress.

"Rumor has it that you princes are seeking a wondrous child said to be born of a God."

"Is that so?"

"Yes, it is no secret. We have known about this at the court for more than a year now. My father, however, forbids any talk of it, for many of the Jews believe that this child will be the next king. My father cannot bear the thought of a rival, and of course he even fears that I might attempt to take the throne."

"What do you want from me?" Melchior asked.

"Is this rumor true? Is there a God-child? Will he be a king? What do your legends tell you? After all, you have not come this great distance merely to visit my father."

"Much of what you say is true, young prince. But I cannot tell you any more than the fact that we are on a mission that we hope can clarify all your questions. Even we do not know whether the child exists. If he does, and I say if, we still don't know where to find him. But if we do find him, then the whole world shall know."

"Be careful not to let my father hear you say that. He is such a dangerous man when he feels threatened. Such an event would threaten him, and he might do something terribly drastic."

"What would you do if we found the child?" Melchior asked quietly.

"I would come and pay my respects to him and seek ways and means of helping him."

"And what if it is your throne that he wants?" Melchior watched his young guest. "After all, you're next in line to the throne after your father."

"I'm not so sure about that," young Herod said. "There is much intrigue at this court. My half-brothers Archelaus and Antipas are also after the throne. Whatever comes, it will be one terrible struggle. Perhaps an outsider would be best for all concerned."

"I cannot tell you anything more," Melchior said. "We do not have much to go on. Thank you for your concern, young Herod."

The dark-haired young prince bowed and left Melchior to finish dressing. The British prince mused and thought about his visitor, but he did not feel good about it—young Herod's warning was ringing in his ears.

In the room where Balthazar lay, Philo had been attending to the black prince's needs.

"That wound is getting no better, my prince," Philo said solemnly. "I must insist that you see a doctor. If you don't, I'm going to tell the others."

"I forbid you to do so," Balthazar said sternly.

"You are in no position to forbid anyone," Philo said, as he cleaned the wound once more. "You cannot go on like this. After all, you are in King Herod's court. Surely he has the best physicians here for healing."

"I wouldn't trust him," Balthazar said, realizing that Philo was correct about the seriousness of the wound.

"Well then, will you permit me to go to the elder Joseph of Arimathea and seek his advice?"

"Only if you do not tell the others."

"Very well. I shall get that physician here under some pretext. After all, you must look your best for the great party and banquet this evening."

The evening activities began with a sumptuous meal. The men had gathered in the library of the palace for a taste of wine. Herod had the very best brought before them. The elder Joseph of Arimathea was there. He had brought his physician on the pretext that a doctor was needed to keep a watchful eye on him. Balthazar seemed to be in the best of spirits. Caspar remained quiet and observant of everything. There was much merriment in the air. Herod, being the kind of crafty man he was, decided to put everyone off guard from the very beginning.

"So, you have come seeking a star, and he who is to be born king of the Jews?" he inquired.

Philo dropped his cup. The others were slightly unnerved.

"But you are king of the Jews," Balthazar said calmly.

"I know that I am." Herod tugged at his curled beard once again. "But there are some around me who say that a Messiah is coming, a savior who will free us from Roman rule and who will set up his kingdom right here in Jerusalem."

"Is that the rumor?" Caspar asked. "But you are the rightful king."

"So I am, but the wise men in my court, along with the religious leaders, have been whispering behind my back about these things for the past five years. They do not think I am aware of them. I am not so stupid as I look. Nor am I so cruel as some would make me seem. I, for myself, would like to see this child-king and would like to pay homage to him. I already know of your studies of the stars. You have probably calculated where he is to be born."

"We only know that it is to be somewhere here in the east,"

Balthazar volunteered. "But have you not noticed the stars, your Majesty?"

"All the stars look alike to me," Herod said, with a wave of his hand. "The only thing that has changed in Jerusalem since I have been king is that I have made of her a more glorious city."

The group moved toward the spacious dining hall. Herod purposefully chose to walk next to Balthazar. "Noble black Prince, we all know you to be a man of integrity. I have a favor to ask of you."

"If I can serve you in any way, your Majesty," Balthazar said cautiously.

Then Herod spoke loud enough for all to hear. "Go your way through the country. Use my name to gain entrance where you must. Seek out this young child, and when you have found him, bring me word, that I also may go and worship him. That way all the world shall know that Herod the Great in the end is as human, as kind, and as willing to live at peace with all mankind as is anyone else."

The dinner itself was glorious. They ate pheasant, lamb, a special kind of goat meat, and a variety of fish. The fruits and vegetables had been grown on the royal farms. In the great dining hall the guests were entertained by magicians with wonderous tricks that the princes had never seen before. There were jugglers, fire-eaters, and dancers. The evening finished with court wrestling. The three princes enjoyed that event most. Melchior only wished that he could have been a contestant. When it was all over, King Herod proposed a toast to the betrothed young couple, wishing them happiness and long life for their coming marriage. "And," he said to his daughter, "may you bear many sons."

When the evening had ended, Balthazar retired to his own room, attended by the elder Joseph and the physician. Once again his wound had to be cleaned and the dressing changed. The doctor looked at the elder nobleman and shook his head. "I don't know. I've never seen a wound like this. It should heal, but I can tell from the tissue that it is getting worse."

"Can it be healed?" Balthazar asked as the doctor was rewrapping it.

"I must tell you the truth, young prince. The wound is feeding on itself. It will continue to grow worse." He paused and sighed deeply. He placed both hands on the young man's shoulders and looked into his deep, dark eyes. "Ultimately of course, you will die."

"I know that," Balthazar said, not sadly, "but how long do I have?"

"It's hard to say, because you are continually losing much blood. Perhaps it is better that you journey back to your homeland. You could spend there what time you have."

"No," Balthazar nearly shouted, "I cannot do that. I must go on. I must complete my task."

"And I," said the doctor, "I have done all that I can do. It is now all in the hands of God."

The day after the banquet, the princes left Herod's palace and returned to the home of the elder Joseph of Arimathea. Balthazar thought this best, for he did not want Herod to know about his wound. Besides, they needed a safe place where they could gather together their forces and then move on to find the holy child.

In the large family room and library of the Arimathean home, the princes, along with Philo and Clitus, gathered with their hosts. Balthazar sat at the head of the table, while the others were sitting at various places about the room.

"We don't have too much time," the black prince told them. "I have asked you all to gather here because we must move and move quickly. I have something that I can no longer keep from you."

"What is it, Balthazar?" Caspar asked, his heart quaking with fear.

"As you know, we had a fierce fight with Nebuchadnezzar to free you, my dear Spanish prince. The night of that fight, I was so anxious to get to you that I forgot to wear the protective iron mesh girdle that Melchior had brought for me. So—"

"So?" Melchior interrupted.

"So my wound has opened. It is a wound that will not heal. Shemhazai told me it would not heal. Therefore, my friends, I am a dying man. But I must live until this most difficult task is completed."

"But you cannot die, my prince, and you cannot go on." Clitus

99

was talking. "Your father the king will hold me responsible if anything happens to you."

"I have already written him a letter explaining everything. You will not be blamed for anything. Now listen to me. We'll have no more talk about my going back. We have come this far with a determined purpose and are going to see it through. You are not to concern yourselves with me. I will live to see the God-child."

Balthazar turned to the older host. "Has Simeon arrived yet?"

"He is here, my prince."

"Then let him come in."

Clitus went to the door as the elder Joseph nodded his head. When the door opened, a small, older man in Jewish dress entered. There was a faded white turban around his head, and he had a long, flowing white beard. With him was also an older woman.

Balthazar turned and spoke to the old man, who bowed before the prince. The woman bowed also.

"Greetings to you, Simeon. Your devotion to your God is known even in my part of the world."

"We all know of the heroic acts of the great Balthazar," replied the old man.

"And who is the woman?" Melchior questioned.

Old Simeon smiled. "You must be Prince Melchior, the prince with the golden hair. She is Anna the prophetess. When the elder Joseph asked me to come to you and told me the nature of your visit, I thought that she would be valuable in any talking we do."

"She is welcome," Balthazar said. "Clitus, provide chairs for our guests."

The two newcomers were added to those around the table. Everyone was alert and anxious to meet the challenge that lay before them.

"Now, we know the God-child is to be born here somewhere in Palestine," Balthazar began. "Our studies of the stars and whatever writings we can find in the scriptures seem to indicate this."

"We think the child has already been born," Simeon said, and his statement startled the princes and their friends.

"Why do you say that?" Melchior asked.

"Because we have seen the star," the old man replied.

"What star?" the British prince asked.

"The star that announced his birth. It was a star which burned so brightly that night almost looked like day."

"But not everyone has seen this star," Caspar exclaimed. "And in Herod's court such a star has been denied. No one there has seen it."

"No one there can see it," Anna told them firmly. "Their hearts and minds are evil and so they cannot see the star."

"Then who can see it?"

"He that hath clean hands and a pure heart, and he whose soul is not vain," Simeon answered.

"So the star is a matter of the heart," Balthazar mused.

"That it is," the old couple agreed.

"Then I have seen it," Balthazar said.

His two friends gasped. "You've seen it? What do you mean, you've seen it? You didn't tell us anything about it."

The black prince laughed warmly. "My brothers, you must forgive me. I don't tell everything I know. I have seen that star every night since we last saw Shemhazai."

"It is right that the three of you are here," Anna said to them. "I saw you coming in a dream. It is for you to go forth and proclaim this holy child the Messiah. He is indeed God's Son, but unless you reach him before Herod does, he remains in constant danger."

"Where will we find the child?" Melchior asked.

"In Bethlehem. It is the least significant and yet the most beautiful town in all Judea," Balthazar answered. Again his two companions were stunned.

"In Bethlehem of Judea! How in the world did you know?"

"He has known all along," Philo said. "And you two have known also, if you have been paying attention."

"That's right." Caspar snapped his fingers. "Of course. Don't you remember, Melchior, we found in the Hebrew scriptures that reference to Bethlehem being the least of all the cities of Judah, yet out of her would come a governor?"

"I'll be a tree wolf!" the blue-eyed prince declared.

"I would make a request of the great Balthazar," Simeon said.

"Speak, and it shall be granted," the black prince assured him.

"Anna and I are old. We shall die soon and go to our fathers. God has promised both of us that we shall see the glory of Israel before we die. We have seen the child in our dreams, but no one has come to proclaim him. Permit us to go with you so that we shall be able to see this great thing done."

"It shall be done," Balthazar said.

"I would like to go also," young Joseph told Balthazar.

"It would be selfish of us to refuse you. Please come along as our companion."

That evening, when the princes had retired to their own quarters, they spoke among themselves.

"I'm not worried about young Joseph," Melchior said, "but won't the older people slow us up?"

"They may," Balthazar said, "but I don't see how we can deny their request. We owe them so much."

"The way to Bethlehem will take us through some dangerous country, won't it?" Caspar asked.

"Begging your pardon, my prince," said Clitus. "But at Herod's palace I learned that there is an evil bandit roaming the hill and desert country between here and there."

"Who is this bandit?" Caspar asked, feeling for his sword.

"His name is Barabbas, and he has a devil of a son by the same name. They say the lad isn't twelve years old, yet he rides and handles the bow like a man."

"Then we must take very careful precautions," Balthazar said. "I don't want another encounter with bandits, but we can't always know what will happen at any given time."

"What will you do when we find the child?" Melchior wanted to know. "Herod asked you to bring him word. Will you do it?"

The black prince smiled. His pearly teeth shone in his strong mouth. "What do you think? I know a fox when I see one."

"Then you will not return to tell him."

"Caspar, I doubt that I shall return at all."

No sooner had Balthazar spoken these words than he leaned forward, his head falling against the table with a hard thud.

"Quick, Clitus! Bring the doctor, and warm water with clean cloths."

Melchior lifted the black prince and carried him over to his bed. He and Caspar loosened his clothes and tried to make him as comfortable as possible.

"Is he still breathing?" a worried Caspar asked.

"Barely."

"My God," cried Caspar. "He cannot die just now. Not now!"

The doctor came as quickly as he could. He bathed the wound, poured some oil and wine into it, and wrapped it tightly to halt the flow of blood. Then gently he turned Balthazar over and poured some liquid medicine into his mouth.

The black prince slept calmly through the night. When morning came he looked pale and weakened. Nonetheless, he decided that they should move on. In order to save his strength, Balthazar sat in the family room with Simeon, Anna, and Philo, while Caspar, Melchior, and the others made things ready. Balthazar did not talk very much. Anna sat silently praying and asking God to give the black prince the strength needed for the journey that lay ahead. Philo and Simeon talked in whispered tones about the history of Israel and its relation to this one true God. The talk itself was quite an experience for the old teacher. He was thrilled and overjoyed at what he was learning. Simeon proved to be an exceptional teacher himself. They reviewed the story of the nation, how it had been born and created through its father Abraham, and how the twelve tribes that made up the nation came from the twelve sons of Jacob. Each of these tribes had a specific function within the nation of Israel. Israel itself was to be a light unto the non-Jewish world and would point the way to this one God, who really desired to be made known unto all men in all lands, everywhere.

Simeon continued, pointing out that the people of the nation became wicked and forgot the God who had blessed them, and went off to their own evil ways. Even after serious punishments they would not return to God. This disturbed God, for soon his Son, the Messiah, or savior, was going to be born as a man.

Blue sky, high white clouds, no air stirring at all, heat unbearable, sweat flowing freely from skin to clothes to animal to ground —the journey was on its way. Caspar was in command of everything, because Balthazar found it difficult even to get up and walk around. He had lost so much blood that there was little that he had strength to do. In fact, he had barely awakened when the bleeding started again. Everyone was fearful, but no one dared to speak or even suggest that they not go on. Balthazar had made his position clear, and everyone understood this. Caspar and Melchior checked on him every other hour, and they moved forward as comfortably as they could with as much speed as could be allowed. But, as they traveled, leaving Jerusalem far behind, they did not know that the great king Herod had already learned about their plans. In fact, the night before their departure, when they had been tending to Balthazar, the Jewish monarch, toying with his curled beard, was holding an audience with his ministers and court.

"All we know is that they have not yet found the child." He strode up and down impatiently. "They only know what you know: The child will be Hebrew, as myself, and yet not be a member of the royal family." The wise men and ministers cringed before the great Herod. They were all afraid of him and his power. "Yet not one of you, the wisest and greatest of wise men and counselors, not one of you is able to tell me where this child is to be born. What am I surrounded by? A group of idiots! Even the children in our temple schools know more than you."

"We know that Balthazar's caravan heads for Judea."

"Judea is nothing but a stopping-off place for jackals and vultures," the king growled. "No king in his right mind would be born there."

"But we know they are headed there."

"The only thing they are bound to meet is the bandit Barabbas. And it would serve them right if they should meet and fight and kill each other. That way we would be rid of two sources of trouble. I have heard nothing but talk of a Messiah since the star appeared that you told me about. A star that I have not yet seen, mind you. A star that most of you have not seen. I rule over a kingdom of guessers and stargazers, but no one knows anything. Well, maybe I'll rid myself of all this nonsense once and for all. I have let Barabbas know that a caravan with three very rich princes is headed his way. The outcome should prove interesting."

"What if they should meet Barabbas and are killed?" asked one of the courtiers.

"That is no problem. It only means that they shall not be a threat to me or to my throne."

"But what if they get through and find the child?" another asked.

"Then we shall go and pay our respects to the child." Herod's grin was deeply evil. "We shall pay homage to him and cut his throat."

The men of the court retreated in fear of their king.

In the meantime, Anna and Simeon talked in whispering tones as they ate dinner together.

"I feel for tomorrow," the woman said to the old man.

"In what way?"

"I feel that the travelers will be in peril. It is as though the devil himself is out to stop us. The whole host of hell is determined that we should not get through."

"I know," nodded the old man. "My bones feel the same way. Yet I know that we can't turn back. Somehow we must go on and do what has to be done."

"And what of the young black prince?"

"I fear for him, Anna. He gets weaker and weaker."

"Yet he has such strong faith, and to think that he is not even one of our people."

"Maybe his faith makes him one of our people. At least he is one with us in our cause and our hopes for the world."

"He is such a brave soul. I am sure that God will open Paradise to receive such a brave one."

"I think we do well to pray that he may reach the end of this journey. It is sure that he will not make another."

"It was wise of him to know of the star being in Bethlehem, wasn't it?"

"He was correct about its shining in the heart. Not every man can see the star, and that's what makes me love this black prince so. He is a foreigner, yet he has seen the star in his own heart."

...
viii

THE NIGHT WAS COOL AND CALM. MELCHIOR AND CASPAR STOOD watch together. In silence they scanned the heavens, looking and marveling as they always did about the vast number and varied arrangements of the stars. That particular night, however, was different without being different, transformed and yet the same. The very air itself was filled with expectation. Somehow each of them knew that they were coming at last to the end of their long quest. Confidence flowed through them like the warmth of good wine. From time to time they looked in on Balthazar, who seemed to be sleeping more and more, without any improvement whatsoever. Balthazar's continually weakening condition worried them. If he should die before they reached their destination, the memories of him would always be sad ones.

"We would know the God-child," Melchior said, "but somehow it would not be the same as if it were Balthazar who proclaimed him."

"His prayers and courage have led us so far; we have to keep him alive until we get there," Caspar said. And in his eyes, Melchior saw that the Spanish prince was already accepting the fact of Balthazar's death.

Toward the cool of the early morning, when night begins to change place with day, both princes began to grow heavy with sleep. Just as they were drifting off, Caspar nudged Melchior sharply with his elbow. His arm drew a long upward line which ended at the fingertip.

"Do you see what I see?" he asked, wearily rubbing his eyes.

Melchior's voice got caught in his throat. "It cannot be true. We've been out here all night and we haven't seen it."

"Yet there it is!" Caspar shouted. "It's the star, the blessed star, the very star we've been looking for."

"It is the most beautiful, glorious, heavenly sight I have ever seen." Melchior's eyes flooded with tears.

Caspar fell to the ground on his knees. He rubbed his eyes again. Never before had either of them seen a star so brilliant, with such radiant lights. Each light was as bright as the others; and, all in all, the star cast toward the earth the six colors of Balthazar's six angels: white, red, green, gold, black, and blue. Even the black part of the star shone and was clear to them. For the longest time, as they knelt reverently, they could not move.

Then a second miracle occurred. As the sun began to rise in the east, the holy star did not disappear as the other stars did. Rather, it still shone, and even though it was not as bright, or did not seem as bright, as it had been in the dark, yet it was still there to beckon them onward to proclaim the Son of God.

Slowly the camp began to stir. People were gathering beside a slow-moving stream in order to wash themselves and prepare for breakfast. Suddenly there were sharp cries of angry, evil men. Their shouts split the peace and calm of the early-morning air. The harrowing sight of war horses charging through the camp froze their bodies in fear. Without a second thought, Caspar grabbed his sword and shield and ran from his tent. Melchior clutched his sword, bow, and leather pouch of arrows and sprang toward the swarming horde of bandits. Dirt, dust, and death flew everywhere. At least ten men from the caravan lay on the ground with their heads split open. Some had deep gashes in their necks. Two had even lost their heads. Caspar ran into the thick of the battle, swinging his sword like a club. He made every stroke count. Melchior was right behind him. They could see Clitus and their personal servant-bodyguards coming to aid them. The noise and fury of the battle echoed for miles around. In all the turmoil of a fierce, fiery, clashing encounter, it was hard for the princes to tell who the leader was. It was also difficult for the men from the caravan to defend themselves adequately, for they had been cut off from their weapons by the surprise attack.

"I must open up a way so our men can get to their weapons!" Melchior shouted to Caspar, slipping off his bow.

"All right, I'll try to get to a horse!" Caspar was a demon soldier upon a horse. He could maneuver more swiftly on horseback than he could on the ground.

Melchior began to shoot his arrows. Thwack! The first one found its mark. Thump! A bandit rider dropped, an arrow piercing his neck. Melchior spun to avoid a sword blow and shot from his knees. Zing! The arrow struck another bandit, who fell to the ground. Melchior could load his bow and shoot it faster than anyone had ever seen. True to his word, he was opening up a space so that his men could get through to their weapons. Because of the fury of his bow, the bandits began to give ground a little. More of the men of the caravan could fight now, and the battle began to even up. Melchior's arrows kept flying, and Caspar's sword kept reflecting the sun as if sending some strange kind of cryptic flash-on, flash-off message. Clitus fought hard, bravely, and strongly. He had been cut on the arm but had not felt it. Philo had fallen under a cart and thought it best to stay there. Scholars and teachers have no reason to fight, he assured himself. As one of Melchior's arrows fell near him, he said aloud, "Wish he knew what side he was on. That was too close."

As the battle entered its second hour, the men began to fight more intensely. It was like a grand wrestling match. Some were on the ground, others were standing up. Wherever they could, men on both sides used the short knife. Sounds of pain, surprise, and death still came. For a while it looked as if neither side would win or lose. Then suddenly there was a blood-chilling shout.

"Hear me, O hear me, you three noble princes!" It was the voice of Barabbas. "Hear me, ye three princes. This is Barabbas speaking!"

The noise and tumult began to die down.

"Someone is trying to speak to us," Caspar shouted to Melchior.

The voice came again. "This is Barabbas. Listen to me. I want to speak to you. Let us shed no more blood. Let there be an end to the killing."

The scene grew even quieter. Men began to stop their fighting.

"I want to make a deal with you. I want to talk."

"Who are you and what do you want?" shouted Melchior.

"I am Barabbas. I am the great bandit warrior. I want to talk."

"We have nothing to talk about," Melchior shouted back.

"Yes, we do. I have the old woman, Anna, the holy one. And I also have holy Simeon. If you do not talk with me, they will die."

"Is he telling the truth?" Caspar asked.

"Clitus, check their tents and tell me."

Clitus ran off quickly in the direction of the tents belonging to their guests.

"I'll bet Herod put him up to this," Caspar muttered to Melchior.

"I'd bet the same thing."

"What are we going to do?"

"If he has really captured them, there is nothing we can do. We'll have to talk with him."

"I can already guess what he wants."

"We know what he wants."

Clitus raced back with his answer. "They are not in their tents, nor have they been seen."

"All right, Barabbas, we'll talk. What do you want?" Melchior shouted.

"I want the treasure you are carrying for this king."

"We have no treasure," Caspar shouted. "We have only several small gifts."

"They would be of no value to you," Melchior added.

"They will bring me a king's ransom. Herod wants them. That's why I'm here." His laughter rang out across the rugged terrain. The two princes looked at each other, not knowing what to do.

Caspar thought quickly. "We'll give you two hostages instead. Let us continue on in peace. Name your price and we'll return with it in exchange for the lives of the hostages."

"No!" shouted the outlaw. "I want that treasure and I intend to have it."

"What do we do now?" Caspar asked.

In the next few moments Barabbas showed himself. He was well over six feet tall, with long matted hair and shoulders as broad as any of his fiercest bandits. He had the stride and strength of a great lion. He ordered the two older people thrown to the dirt in front of him.

"Don't listen to him," Anna cried weakly, trying to shout.

"We are ready to die," Simeon added. "Your mission must continue."

The bandit kicked at the couple lying prostrate in front of him. "I told you to be quiet!" he roared. "Well, my sweet princes, what do you say? Do I get the treasure or do these fine old holy people die? I'll give you only five moments to make up your minds."

"We won't need that five moments!" another voice shouted.

Caspar and Melchior looked at each other. They recognized the voice even though they could not believe their ears. Their heads turned and their eyes looked. Before them, in full battle dress, stood Balthazar!

"Hear me, O Barabbas, hear me and fear me! You will set those two holy people free. You will take your rabble and get out of here while there is yet time. Otherwise I shall personally take pleasure in removing your wild head from your body."

"Ha! ha! black one," Barabbas shouted. "I know that you are wounded and are dying. You are no match for me when you are well. Fighting you would be like putting a lame horse out of its misery."

"I'm sure you would not like to find that I still carry the sting of a scorpion. Now take your rabble and go. Enough good men have died this day because of you."

"I will not go unless I get what I came for. Either you surrender the treasure or you shall see these two people lose their heads."

Balthazar moved straight and tall toward the robber. Caspar and Melchior were struck dumb. Balthazar stood midway between them, his footing unstable in the desert sands.

"Since I am wounded, Barabbas, I will make a deal with you."

"What is that, black one?"

"I am wounded, as you say. But I indeed know you to be a coward and a beater of old women and children. Fight me for the treasure. Slay me, and you shall have it. Let your sword and mine decide alone who shall keep the treasure."

"Do I have your word?"

"You have my word and my oath as a prince of the Royal House of Har'lem."

"He is not himself," Melchior whispered. "We have to stop him."

"I wouldn't like to try, if I were you," Caspar told him.

Evil laughter mingled with the quiet blowing sand. Barabbas shouted in the direction of his men. "Let all eyes rest upon me! Never will you see a treasure so easily won. I hope you have a priest in your caravan, black one. He can pray over you at the bleeding of your final wound. I intend to kill you quickly."

"Let us stop talking," Balthazar shouted at him. "I'm ready."

"We have to stop him," Melchior said, jumping to his feet. "No, Balthazar!" he cried. "You are in no condition to meet this vulgar beast. Let me do it. I'll slice his belly open and create a first-class delight for the vultures."

"Fear not, kind Melchior. Let him come after me and see what a sick man can do. He can do nothing but add to the legend of Balthazar. In fact, my brother, lend him your sword. Let him know what it is like to die with a royal sword in his hand."

A fierce, cold heat burned in Balthazar's eyes. His body seemed to become calm in the midmorning sun. His breathing was natural enough, but Caspar's keen eyes could already see that the blood was beginning to seep through the costume of the fighting prince. Melchior handed his sword to the proud Barabbas. The bandit took it in his hand and stabbed the air with it once or twice. The men who stood around now came to attention as the two adversaries faced each other.

Sensing that the moment had come, Balthazar took the lead by moving first. He crept in on Barabbas, who was somewhat unnerved by this dying man who crouched before him. Balthazar's eyes never left those of his opponent. The two men circled slowly,

112

trying to size each other up. Barabbas lunged forward and Balthazar moved out of his way simply by turning with ease. The thief leaped forward again. This time the swords of the two fighters clashed and locked at the hilts. Barabbas thought he would be stronger and therefore could push Balthazar back and down to the ground with ease. His plan worked. The knees of the great black warrior buckled, and he fell to the ground on his back. Melchior and Caspar jumped up from where they had been sitting frowning with worry and fear for their already wounded comrade.

The swords of the fighters were still locked, and the bandit used all his strength to continue forcing and pushing Balthazar's sword closer to his neck. The black prince felt the warm sand pushing against his back. He thought that he was using all the strength he had. He did not realize how weak he had become. Sweat poured from his face as he writhed under the weight of the giant Barabbas. For a moment his brain felt furry inside and his thoughts did not come clearly. Then, summoning all the strength that he could, he simply used an old soldier's trick and rolled over, making Barabbas' forced strength work against him. Balthazar was now on top. He could not press the sword to the chieftain's throat, so he immediately jumped to his feet and moved back. "Help me, O one true God. Make those who watch this day know that you are in truth the defender of all those who put their trust in you."

Barabbas moved in on Balthazar again. This time he swung with intent. The prince met his blow and thrust back with another, which Barabbas dodged with ease. They lunged and side-stepped again and again, until Barabbas' great strength brought victory within his grasp. Balthazar had everything he could do to keep his head upright and think. Suddenly he slumped and tripped, falling to the ground. The snarling Barabbas ran toward him, shouting, with upraised sword. He did not see or sense the small rock beneath his foot that sent him falling wide. As he fell, Balthazar took a handful of sand and threw it into the bandit chief's eyes. Barabbas turned his head in a blind rage, leaving his chest open, so that he did not feel all at once Balthazar's sword as it pierced through him. He thrashed like a man blinded with drink. Then the pain hit him. His hands went up to grasp at the sword that lay embedded in his large chest. He yelled and screamed like a wounded animal, but there was no hope for him. His men began to gather themselves together and already some of them were stealing off. The blood began to flow now. It dripped from both the front and the back of his massive body where Balthazar's sword had done its work. Barabbas roared like a lion, turned his head up in the direction of the sun and died.

Relief, quickly followed by concern, flowed through the camp. Relief that Balthazar had won and the treasure was saved; concern that the black and shining prince now also fell forward onto the sand and did not move. Caspar and Melchior ran as fast as they could to their fallen comrade's side.

"Is he dead?" Clitus asked Melchior, who held him.

"He's unconscious. Quick, let's make him comfortable. Someone fetch the doctor."

Again, Clitus ran off as fast as he could, stumbling over himself as he went. He found the doctor and returned with him. Old Anna prepared and heated water to bathe the wound. Old Simeon brought the clean cloths from where they had been stored. It took the better part of an hour to tend to Balthazar. As the doctor and the two older people worked, Caspar did what he could to get the camp in readiness so that they could move out as quickly as possible. Melchior took the sword out of the body of Barabbas and went down to the stream to wash it. There he noticed a half-grown boy whose face was dirty and whose eyes were tear-streaked.

"Who are you, boy? Why did you not flee like the others?"

"The black prince killed my father."

"Your father?" Melchior was surprised.

"Yes," came the answer. "Barabbas was my father. I hope the prince does not die. I don't want him to die."

Melchior missed the bitterness in the boy's tone of voice. "We don't want him to die either."

"But our reasons are different. I want him to get better and to heal. I want him to live so that someday, when I am older, I can seek him out. I swear I will kill him in the same way he killed my father."

"But your father was a thief," Melchior told him.

"My father was a man," the boy answered, wiping new tears

from his eyes. "And I swear that as he took my father away from me, so shall I one day take him away from his sons."

"What is your name?" Melchior asked him.

"The same as my father's. Barabbas."

The sun climbed higher into the sky. The day was not at all cool. Balthazar was resting comfortably on a litter drawn by two horses, and shaded by cloths stretched over supports. The black prince, however, had not regained consciousness. As the caravan moved along its way, there was little feeling of happiness through it. Already the journey had been too costly.

"He can last only one more day," the doctor had told them. "That fight took too much out of him."

"There's nothing more you can do?" Melchior asked.

"You'll have to bury him tomorrow." The doctor was grave and sad.

"How far are we from Bethlehem?" Melchior asked old Simeon.

"I'd say we were a full day and a half journey."

"You mean that we can't get there until tomorrow at sunset?" Caspar asked.

"There is no way," Anna told them.

"But the doctor says that Balthazar will die before then. What can we do?" Melchior's voice was weak with desperation.

"There's nothing for you to do," replied the old woman. "Men measure time by the sun. The God whom we serve measures time by his own breath."

"We can't go back and we can't go forward, yet we must make a choice," Philo observed.

"We'll do what Balthazar would want us to do." Caspar had made up his mind. "We'll go forward and we'll trust in this God."

"You have learned well. You carry the courage of the black prince and the faith of the world's holy men," said Simeon, trying to encourage Caspar.

They traveled as far as they could that day without shaking Balthazar too much. They made camp on the top of a high plateau where, out in front of them, stretched vast plains. They could see off in the far, far distance the towns that were along the route to Bethlehem. Among the soldiers and the servants there was

115

unaccustomed quiet. Caspar did not understand why, but he too did not feel much like talking. Melchior sat alone gazing off into space. It was a strange evening for each prince. Each felt that he should be sad, yet there was no room for sadness. Something holy was happening in their minds and bodies.

Anna helped prepare the evening meal for those who were not among the soldiers or second-rank guards. Young Joseph of Arimathea, who had done well in his first battle, helped her. Simeon and the elder Joseph recited evening prayers together. The meal itself was simple fare, yet hearty and filling. Everyone served everyone else with confidence and contentment.

After supper, Clitus was the first to notice a strange, sweet sound that seemed to be coming to them on the wind.

"What do you suppose that is?" Melchior asked. They were far away from any rocks or streams that might cause the sound of an echo.

"I have no idea," Caspar said.

"I've never heard anything like it," young Joseph of Arimathea told them. "Never in my lifetime."

"Look over there, toward the east," Philo said, amazed.

Although the sky around and over them was darkening into a velvety blue-black, off in the distance it held on to a reddish-orange glow. The longer they looked at it, the warmer in color it grew. The red and yellow seemed to merge, and then out of the cool night came a heavenly blue and green to merge with it. It spun in a circular motion that seemed to go in all directions at one time. Soon white and gold were added to the glowing lighted mass. All eyes watched in awe at this sight, for now everyone could see it. And then, though it was impossible, and though no one could believe it, the color black, of purest night, was added to it all; and the whirling mass seemed to catch fire and glow as if it were a special piece of God's firewood burning in his great sky. It even sent out sparks, so that the whole of heaven was aglow.

"Nobody's going to make me believe that Herod can't see that!" Melchior shouted.

"He can't see it," Anna told him. "He's a proud and vain man who does not recognize God, so this sight is kept from his eyes."

"Then Balthazar was correct," Caspar exclaimed for joy. "He has seen this sight all along."

"Yes, he has seen it, and so have a few of the chosen of us. Perhaps it is better that more than one or two of us see it. This way, the truth of it can be established. We are all witnesses together."

"Then all our studies have not been in vain," Caspar said.

"No, they have not," Simeon told the young prince. "You were prompted by something inside you that is inside every man. You simply had eyes to see, ears to hear, and a heart to receive it all."

Caspar knelt facing in the direction of the star. He let his forehead touch the cool, cool sand. The others followed his example. The sound of the wind became clearly musical, as though a hundred golden harps were being plucked by a hundred magical angelic fingers of green, blue, black, white, red, and gold. As the night grew darker and the star grew brighter, there came voices from the direction of the star and the heavens, voices singing songs so beautiful and so strange that those in the caravan thought themselves either to be dreaming or dying. Finally, about midnight, closer to their own camp, they saw what they thought was a smaller version of that same star. It whirled and twirled around them, shooting off its heavenly sparks. It came closer and closer and grew bigger and bigger. The hearts of all who were in the caravan quivered in awe. They all saw themselves as dying, for no one had seen such a wondrous and glorious sight before. The voices grew louder and the light grew brighter. The sound seemed to say something like "Hallelujah! Hallelujah! Hallelujah!" Scarcely had they heard this when a great whirring noise, louder then a swarm of locusts, sounded in their ears. All of a sudden, this whirling light that had been coming toward them spilled down, rolled over, and broke into a living chorus of a thousand singing angels. The voices and colors swirled and blended, cascaded and showered around them until poor Anna thought her heart would surely stop.

"Fear not, fear not!" said a tall, black shimmering angel. "Behold, we bring you good tidings of greatest joy."

A green angel stepped to the fore. "Unto you is born, and is alive this day, in David's city, a savior."

"This child is God's Son," proclaimed the red angel.

"His name is Jesus, but he shall be called Christ: the Christ of God," the gold angel told them.

"This shall be a sign unto you," the blue angel announced. "You shall find the child living in simple surroundings, playing in a manger."

"Hurry!" said the white angel. "Hurry! Herod will not be long behind you. See the child, proclaim him, and then provide him safe passage with his mother and father into Egypt."

Abruptly, without warning, the whole band of angels came together and swelled up into one sudden force of bright, bright light, nearly blinding the watchers. And they went back into the sky, flying out toward the holy star. They continued to sing and praise God who had made heaven and earth and all humankind. They also pronounced peace upon all who seek good will.

There never before was a day like that on the face of the whole earth, and there has never been such a day since.

ix

No one slept much that night of nights. Early the next morning they all started out for Bethlehem, where of course the star had been all the time. Balthazar was deeply asleep, showing almost no signs of life. Even so, the friendly winds seemed to whisper that it was a wondrous day. No one spoke, or seemed to have need of speaking. They just went along, everyone in his own way. Even the soldiers were astonished. They did not feel like men of war, they simply felt like men. For many of them it was the first time in their lives. They too heard the wind and were guided in peace by its gentle calling. The sand suddenly seemed transformed and they all felt as though they were on a huge boat that was drawing them near to the place where they would find the Christ-child. Even Simeon and Anna felt as though they were young people again, as if perhaps they would fall in love for the first time.

The caravan did not pause to eat that day, for no one seemed hungry. Late in the afternoon, just before the sun began to dip in the west, they could see the outlines of the city. And, as the day before, the star seemed to awaken and grow in beauty a little while before the sun went down. Rays of radiant gold light streamed out toward the horizon and their journey's end just beyond.

The city of Bethlehem was quiet and small compared to Jerusalem. It was the kind of place that bandits left alone because most of the people there were poor. They didn't have riches and treasures, as did inhabitants of large cities on the trade routes. It was a peaceful place. As the travelers came nearer, it seemed as though the events of the night before were ready to repeat themselves. The wind began to hum and moan just as it had done the previous day. Even the sands joined in the song. The city itself, amazingly enough, did not seem to notice. The craftsmen and other merchants went about their ways as on any other day. When the caravan was near enough to the city, Caspar sent Clitus ahead to find what it was they were looking for. Young Joseph wanted to go along, so permission was granted.

"You'll know his birthplace," the Spanish prince told them. "For the star should stand right above it."

The two young men rode off and the camp settled down to wait. Caspar and Melchior went to look at Balthazar. His skin had changed color. He was barely breathing and he looked like death itself. I hope he lasts, they both thought.

Clitus and young Joseph returned and led them around the city to a small house, which was not a very rich-looking one. In fact, it was very simple. It had only two small rooms for cooking, eating, and sleeping. There was a yard with some animals milling around in it. Yet the whole place seemed to give off the air of being a palace. It was clean and magically colorful. It gave everyone who came near it the feeling of being very, very special. The whole caravan stopped in front of the house, but no one knew exactly what to do. As they paused, a young woman came out. She was beautiful to look at. Her dark-brown hair fell like a warm breeze over her youthful face.

"Would you like water for your animals?" she asked.

"We would, fair lady," Melchior managed to say. "I'm afraid there are quite a number of them."

"We have lots of water." She smiled and the stars danced in her dark eyes. Melchior was embarrassed, because he was conscious of staring at her.

"I'll get some of the men to do it if you'll but show me where," he managed to say when he could stop staring.

She led him around to the back of the small house into the barnyard, where there was a well with a watering trough for animals. "Where have you come from?" she asked.

"From far away," Caspar told her. "We are from distant parts of the world. We have seen the star and so we have come."

"I have been praying for you," she said evenly. "I have told my husband that we must stay here until three men come to us from afar. But there must be one more of you."

"Yes, my lady," Melchior said.

"But where is he?"

"He's asleep in the litter around front."

"We have brought gifts for the child, my lady," Caspar told her. "Where is he?"

"He's inside. Come and see."

The two princes entered the house. It was a humble place, yet its warmth was rich. The simple grace of the whole dwelling overshadowed its plainness. The mother led them over into a corner of the room where they saw the child. He was a happy, smiling baby boy who was sitting up playing noisily in a kind of child's pen. He was bigger and more handsome than the princes could have imagined. He was more than a year old and nearly walking and talking. Caspar looked at the mother. She nodded and he gently touched the child, his face glowing. He picked the child up and the baby immediately played with his long black hair. He smiled as he passed the child to Melchior, who looked at him and silently wept.

"His name is Jesus," said the mother softly. The baby Jesus touched one of the tears on that big rugged face and smiled. Melchior had never felt such personal joy and warmth before.

"But what of the other prince?" the mother asked. "Would he wish to share this moment?"

"Yes, my lady," Melchior answered.

"We are afraid he is dying, if not already dead. Yet were it not for him, we would not have come." Caspar spoke gravely.

"Then we must go and see him," she said, lifting the child from Melchior's arms.

They went out into the night air, which seemed warmed by the breath of angels. The sky and the heavens suddenly made them all feel close. As they neared the litter on which Balthazar lay, for the first time since the fight with Barabbas, the black prince moved. He opened his eyes.

"We're here," Caspar whispered. "We have found the child."

Balthazar gasped in thanksgiving. "Help me sit up," he whispered weakly. Clitus moved quickly to please his master. The mother passed the child to the weakened prince, who had stretched out his determined bronze arms to receive him. The child gazed quizzically at Balthazar, who in turn gazed at him. Presently they both smiled as if they had communicated something secret between themselves. Balthazar looked at the mother and there were tears in her eyes. She sighed as though relieved from some great burden, and then he understood. He pressed the child close to himself, burying his face in the holiest of heads.

"You are the Christ, O wondrous Child. I know it and I feel it with all my being. You are the Son of God, and the King of all kings who have been, who are, and who are yet to come. How great it is that I have seen and embraced you this once before I have died. I pay homage to you."

Tears fell from Balthazar's eyes as from the eyes of all those who watched. Anna and Simeon drew near, for they desired to touch the child. Young Joseph of Arimathea fell on his knees as he held the hands of the small boy in his own. The animals, which had been freed from their harnesses and ropes, began to dance. In their own way they formed a chorus and sang. Balthazar handed the child back to his mother.

"Now I can die in peace." He smiled and lay back on the litter. For a moment he closed his eyes. "Melchior," he called. "The gifts, bring them and open them before the King and his mother."

"Of course, my prince."

Servants brought the chests of gold, frankincense, and myrrh. They opened each one, and the mother smiled in delight and pleasure. At this point her husband Joseph came forward, for he had been feeding and unharnessing the animals with the help of some of the soldiers. The princes and the others greeted him warmly and benevolently.

"Are these the guests we have been awaiting?" he asked his wife.

"Yes, they are the three wise men from afar," she said, warmly linking hands with his.

The animals were still dancing. This time the sheep took up with the camels, and the horses with the donkeys. Most of the people were still on their knees, for they did not know what to do or say.

"Then I can believe what the angel said to me?" asked the mother.

"Yes, you can believe it," Caspar told her. "We have come here to tell you . . ."

"To tell you that he is the Christ, the Son of God, the King of Heaven's Armies," a voice broke in.

All eyes turned in surprise toward the litter. Balthazar was sitting up, strong and large. He was smiling and the color of life had come back to him.

"I have now proclaimed him the Son of God," said the black prince. He stood solidly on his own two feet. "Look at me, I am healed. Touching the Child has healed the wound that would not heal. I am once more made whole. He is truly the Christ."

"Our Lord and our God," sighed Anna. "Now, Simeon, you and I can go to our fathers in peace. God has let us see his salvation for the world."

"We are grateful to you, Almighty God of our fathers," Simeon said with his face toward the heavens.

Balthazar turned toward his men. "Let us make camp," he said. "We shall stay here for a few days and then return to our own lands and proclaim to everyone this wonder which we have seen."

Melchior stepped forward, embraced the black and shining prince and kissed his bronzed ebony cheek. "Without you, my black brother, none of this could have happened. Hail to you, O Balthazar, for you are a true prince of peace."

Caspar embraced Balthazar as well. "Hail to you, O brother of mine. Praise be to the God who healed you and brought you back to us."

Then, as the true black prince of Har'lem, kneeling reverently, Balthazar said, "Let us humble ourselves in prayer that we may be found worthy of this greatest of all blessings to men."

"Lord, we offer up to you prayers of praise and thanksgiving for your matchless goodness unto us. We are grateful that you have brought us to this very moment in the history of time. How blest we are to have seen and participated in the birth and life of your good news to the whole world. In return for these and other special blessings we offer unto you our hearts, souls, minds, and our very lives. May we continue in the joy of service unto you and all mankind. Grant us mercy as we make our way back to our homelands. We thank you for the warmth and loyalty of friends, without whom we could not have made this pilgrimage.

"We bless you for wise Philo and his teaching; for our royal fathers and their trust; for Shemhazai and her prophecies; for good Clitus and our loyal soldiers in their faithfulness to us. We give thanks to you for Anna and Simeon in their holy trust; for the elder Joseph and his son in their friendship; and for the many signs and wonders you have shown us all along the way. Lastly, I am grateful for the love and friendship of my brother princes, Caspar and Melchior. May we ever continue to be of service to one another and to comfort one another. We claim your promise to keep us in perfect peace because our minds are fastened on you. By the grace and for the sake of that Holy Child, your Son, our Lord, we offer prayer. Amen."

Balthazar came to his feet. His eyes were moist and his heart and soul were filled. He felt better than he could remember.

Then the whole human chorus shouted together jubilantly, "Hail to Balthazar, Hail to the Christ-child, Hail to the Lord!"

Several days later they broke camp. Balthazar instructed a small group of soldiers to provide safe conduct to young Joseph of Arimathea and to the old holy couple, Anna and Simeon. Because of Herod's treachery, the princes volunteered to take the young child and his parents into Egypt, where Jesus would be safe. Having done all these things, they returned happily to their own lands, where they proclaimed the Christ-child to be King and Lord. And in that way, Christmas was spread all over the world.